THE PEPPERSALT LAND

by Marilyn Harris

FOUR WINDS PRESS NEW YORK

Published by Four Winds Press
A Division of Scholastic Magazines, Inc., New York, N.Y.

Printed in the United States of America
Library of Congress Catalogue Card Number: 70-124189

For Karen and her generation, with love and hope.

ONE

THEY FOUND A SKULL.

Tollie spotted it first, a patch of white sticking up out of a tangle of green vines and brown fallen leaves. Slocum lagged a few feet behind, behaving badly considering that the day had been her idea.

"Slocum, look!" Tollie gasped. Through the shadows, between the bright sun spaces, she could see her friend hanging back. They were coming toward a place in the Peppersalt Land where the trees were high and thick, and moss hung down in long fingers.

"It's nothing," Slocum murmured rapidly. "Just

a broken plate. Come on, let's go back." In all of Slocum's twelve years, her grandmother had given her one rule over and over again: "Never go into the Peppersalt Land." Now she was here. And she was frightened. She inched to one side in an effort to see the white patch that she knew was not a broken plate. In one of these slight movements, her foot cracked a twig. Slocum immediately jumped back, put both hands over her eyes which flooded with tears from the fright, and begged Tollie with all her might, "Please, let's go back," and went down on her knees in a huddle, and could only blurt out through her tears, "I take back everything I said. All of it."

Tollie stared, as if startled by the pitiful figure of Slocum with her tearstained face, disheveled hair and cutoff jeans, below which the white scars caused by bramble bushes could be seen on her legs. She seemed unable to think of anything to say, except maybe admit that she was scared, too. "There's a sissy for you, a crybaby," she said, walking back to the fallen Slocum, gently prodding her with her foot. "You dared me to come in here. Please get up."

"That's not a broken plate over there," cried Slocum. "That's—" and turning away, she hid her face behind her hands.

It was white, peering up close to the trunk of a tree. The girls saw two hollows where the eyes had been. Then there was a bird, slanting and tilting on it. The bird flapped its wings on the white forehead. Tollie glanced back at Slocum.

"Come on," she said. "It can't hurt us none." She looked with compassion on her summer-time friend who crouched on the cool dirt floor of the Peppersalt Land.

Slocum raised her eyes, and tried very hard to summon forth new courage. "All right," she said, still sniffling, but making an attempt to dry her tears. "Every summer that I've been coming to Budding Grove, we've been telling ourselves that this year we're going into the Peppersalt Land. But we'd never do it. Well, now we have. So, let's go."

After Slocum's brave speech, she suddenly fell silent, and it grew so quiet in the tangle of brush and trees that the only sound to be heard was the broken breathing from her own leftover tears. At that moment Slocum was certain that this was the worst thing that had ever happened to her. It occurred to her that she was probably crying less from the fear of real danger than because of all the stories she had heard about the Peppersalt Land. At least she hoped this was the case. Both girls had heard these stories from everyone, from their grandmother, from the Jacksons who lived down the road, from old Mr. Cicero who ran the store at the crossroads that led into Budding Grove, from Slocum's mother and father, especially from her father.

Now Slocum raised up, her face smudged with dirt that had mingled with her tears. "Grandmother told us not to come in here," she pleaded. "But you oughtn't to have said what you said last night. Now, let's go." She scrambled to her knees, and looked as if she were getting ready to start a race.

The two girls stared at one another, each remembering the night before when they had lain together in the big four-poster bed in the second-floor bedroom, whispering and giggling as they had done every summer for as long as they could remember. Then Tollie had said such an awful thing. Just thinking about it made Slocum mad all over again.

"You need a handkerchief," said Tollie, and she sat down flat on the ground, as if to say that she had no intention of leaving for a long time.

"I don't have one," snapped Slocum angrily, and sniffed hard and wiped her hands across her eyes.

Slocum looked into Tollie's face, and was touched by a sorrow unknown to her. She didn't want to be rude, and she was sorry that she and Tollie had argued the night before. But the whole summer had been filled with a foreboding that she couldn't understand. She dared to relax a bit, and looked around at the shady level spot near the foot of the tall tree where the skull lay half-buried.

Tollie ventured nearer and squatted close beside her. "Are you going to tell the Grandmother?" she asked.

"Tell her what?" replied Slocum, wishing that Tollie would just say Grandmother instead of THE Grandmother. Had Tollie said THE Grandmother last summer? Slocum couldn't remember. Everything seemed to add to her confusion, and nothing gave her a clear understanding of what her sorrow was.

"About—that," Tollie said, and pointed toward the skull. She scooted closer, sweat forming tiny rivers on her smooth skin.

It seemed to Slocum there was nothing more important than this moment, and with the idea of reinstating Tollie as her best and only friend, she touched her hand, and smiled. "No, it won't hurt her not to know."

Now they were quiet for a moment, each studying the forbidden surroundings, their eyes carefully avoiding the white patch that rested several yards away.

Shortly after lunch they had ventured beyond the last post-oak fence on Grandmother English's property into this ancient territory called the Peppersalt Land. In the days when Slocum's great-great grandfather had owned over four thousand black slaves in Budding Grove, Georgia, the Peppersalt Land had been home to the rebellious ones, the sullen ones, the ones who, according to Slocum's father, had resisted more savagely than others the blessings of a body-destroying job and the security of certain hunger. Nothing ever passed on the overgrown paths that crisscrossed between the collapsed structures that once had served as shelters. No one ever ventured into this immense unmarked cemetery anymore. Its own legend kept it safe and private. Part swamp, part rock, all overgrown with foliage that resembled high jungle walls, the earth here defied cultivated life of any kind to exist. Even the air was dark. Creepers dropped their ropes like the rigging of grounded ships. And black moss hung coarse as thick hair almost entangling a passerby in a noose-like snare. Slocum's eyes grew wide as she remembered the stories she had heard about the Peppersalt Land. Her father had told her that there was quicksand here that could swallow a man in ten minutes, and deadly poisonous snakes the color of the vines. He had told her that blood ran here in the old days, and cannibalism thrived. She thought of her father back in Philadelphia and remembered how he hated these summer visits to Georgia, and always waited until the last week in August, coming down just in time to take Slocum and her mother back to Philadelphia. Her father had told her that eyes that had borne witness to the living history of the Peppersalt Land were never used for ordinary sights again. And ears that had heard the weeping of life as it was lived behind those impenetrable walls of green never seemed to hear the small noises that idle voices make.

According to legend, the slaves had given it the name the Peppersalt Land, claiming that the tears of agony and despair that had been shed within the dark green confines had turned it into a land of salt. So many tears. It was said that the slave women seasoned their food by weeping over the open kettles.

Remembering all this, Slocum heard the summer wind strum the trees overhead, and it seemed to her that the sound of human sighing could be heard. She felt too depressed to talk, and yet she felt that if she didn't say something, she would hide her face and start crying again.

"Tollie," she said, finally. "Promise you'll never say that word again."

"What word?"

"Everything you said last night, about no one but niggers being allowed to set foot in the Peppersalt Land."

Tollie's eyes grew wide with resentment. "I can say anything I want to say anytime I want to say it, Slocum Mason." Her black eyes sparkled. "Nigger! Nigger! Nigger!" she chanted.

"Stop it." cried Slocum.

"I can say it anytime I want to, because I *am* a nigger, and you're not!" Tollie continued.

Slocum felt an ominous burning behind her eyes.

Suddenly Tollie grabbed Slocum's arm and pressed it against hers. "See?" Black. White. Tollie smiled and turned away, a kind of triumph in her look.

Slocum's eyes rimmed with tears. The undefinable sadness she had felt all summer washed over her full force. She knew with a terrible certainty that she should beg Tollie's forgiveness, but she didn't exactly know what to ask forgiveness for. Confused, she bent back her best fingernail until the flesh stung around the quick. "Who called you that—name?" she murmured, taking care to keep her eyes down. "Has Grandmother . . . ?"

"No, not the Grandmother," Tollie replied, quietly.

"And why do you say THE Grandmother?" snapped Slocum. Suddenly she felt unreasonably critical of Tollie.

Apparently the feeling was mutual. Tollie raised up on her knees, her hands clenched against her legs. "Because she's not MY grandmother, that's why."

"She raised you. You've lived in her house all your life."

"That doesn't make her mine." Tollie's voice flared, then fell—"Or me, hers."

Slocum waited in what would have been true fury, if Tollie's rebuff had not contained so much truth. She wondered how it felt not to belong to anyone. Tollie's mother had died when Tollie was born. She had never known her father. Slocum's grandmother had adopted Tollie and taken her into her house and raised her. Still, that didn't mean that they belonged to each other, as Slocum belonged to her mother and father. To belong. It had a good sound; moreover, it meant loved. Slocum stopped thinking about the opposite of loved.

"Who has called you that name?" she asked again, still shocked by the echo of the word that was strictly forbidden in her own family.

Another girl with her gentleness might have let the subject drop, but not Tollie. She giggled and scooped up a handful of dirt.

"Oh, I've heard it lots of time," she smiled, watching the dirt sift down through her fingers. "From old Mr. Cicero for one, talking to some white man from Budding Grove. I was standing outside his store, and he didn't know I could hear."

Slocum felt that she had, perhaps, pushed the subject too far. Mr. Cicero was a good friend of her grandmother's. "But he's never called you that, has he?" she asked pointedly. "To your face, I mean?"

"He will." Tollie looked up, good-humoredly. "Some people don't like me living with the Grandmother. Some people say it isn't natural, that I ought to be living with my own kind, like the Jacksons down the road."

Slocum sat for a time, tongue-tied with resentment. When she was finally able to speak at all, her comfort was, even to her own ears, weak and silly.

"Pay no attention to what some people say," she muttered, trying to put determination into each word.

"I couldn't care less, one way or the other," Tollie said flippantly. She looked out at the shadowy woods, her dark eyes shining with sadness, her look giving Slocum the impression that she cared very much.

"If *I* ever hear them say bad things," Slocum said, "I'll tell them a thing or two."

"You're never going to get that chance." Tollie got to her feet, brushed her hands together, and stooped to brush the dirt off her knees. "Howard Jackson told me that there was two kinds of ears in the world, black ears, and white ears. And when black ears hear perfectly, white ears go stone deaf."

In deep despair, Slocum thought of what she knew about Howard Jackson, which wasn't much. She knew that he was the son of Mary and Spent Jackson who lived down the road from her grandmother, that he went to college in the North somewhere, and that he always looked slightly mad and very unhappy. She felt like telling Tollie not to pay any attention to what Howard Jackson said either, but she didn't. A light breeze wafting through the foliage of the trees, through her hair and over her perspiring face, felt very refreshing. She heard a slight stirring then, and looking up, saw Tollie moving away from her.

"Don't go yet, please," she called.

"Really, I don't want to stay here anymore—it's boring," Tollie said without looking back.

Words such as these, with their dampening effect on the adventure of the afternoon, were extremely unpleasant, the more so because at heart Slocum couldn't help but admit that everything that Tollie had said was true.

She knew herself that not only she and Tollie couldn't go to a movie together in Budding Grove, they couldn't even have a coke together. Now when Grandmother did Saturday errands they sat in the car. And most of the time their activities were confined to the big house and surrounding property. But if Slocum were to reason like that, and ask questions with no answers, she and Tollie would say more and more terrible things to each other. Yet, she thought,

Tollie herself remembers how in the long summer evenings they carried chairs out on the front lawn, turning them into a carriage; how they took turns playing Joan of Arc, another evening Swiss Family Robinson, the scuppernong arbor being the deserted island; and how on hot, still summer afternoons, they got a pan of ice from the kitchen, and took it out beneath the big willow tree, lying on their backs, crunching coldness, seeing faces in the white clouds that drifted slowly across the high blue sky. And how many different adventures they had had on the way, and how gaily and quickly those wonderful summers had passed. If they were to listen to what Howard Jackson and old Mr. Cicero said, there wouldn't be any friendship left at all. And if there were no friends like Tollie, what would be left?

Slocum suddenly remembered that she was alone in the Peppersalt Land with the white skull grinning at her from beneath the blanket of dead leaves. A rustle in the brush behind her caused her heart to contract as she remembered her father's warning that there were deadly snakes here. She scrambled to her feet in horror, crying, "Tollie, wait! Wait for me!"

She heard her voice in echo, bouncing off the dense damp green walls of the Peppersalt Land, heard Tollie somewhere up ahead of her thrashing her way out of the ominous wilderness. But still Slocum stood rooted to the spot.

Fear grew inside her. And sorrow. She cried again, "TOLLIE!"

There was no answer.

TWO

To be suddenly in doubt about the strength and durability of Tollie's friendship was a terrible thing. Slocum loved Tollie; thoughts and memories of her friend had always sustained her during the snowy Philadelphia winters when she had passed the loneliness of the cold dark nights in her small bedroom, dreaming of the summer days to come when she would return to Budding Grove and share the large bedroom at the top of the stairs with Tollie. Her father had teased her on occasion, saying that she was more her mother's southern child than she was his northern one. Whatever Slocum was or wasn't, she was Tollie's friend. And that was that.

What she couldn't understand was why her friendship with Tollie became more and more difficult as they grew older. When they were younger, they had gone everyplace together: to the Farmer's Market that stretched endlessly, fragrantly on the outskirts of Budding Grove; into dress shops with her grandmother in search of new outfits for special occasions; even into the dime store for ribbons, pink for Tollie's dark hair, blue for Slocum's blond hair. But those summers had slipped by, and as both girls grew older the restrictions increased. Slocum realized that this summer she and Tollie had not once ventured any farther than old Mr. Cicero's store at the end of the road. Slocum's grandmother always went into town alone. Even Megs, the housekeeper, was different. Not once had she invited them to go fishing with her at Hunter's Lake.

Slocum's grandmother was known as Mrs. English to her friends and acquaintances in Budding Grove. She had been born in the tall, once grand house that sat well back from the road on the outskirts of town in a deep grove of willow and pine. Remnants of beauty still clung to the old house with its immense veranda and fluted white pillars that stretched the length of the front porch and reminded Slocum of pictures she had once seen in a book about Greek temples. Slocum considered her grandmother the most beautiful woman she had ever seen. Tall and stately, she was slim and carried herself erect in spite of her seventy plus years. When she sat at the head of the dining room table with her snow-white hair piled soft as clouds around her face, her long, slender arms extending out of the palest lavender voile dress, a tiny pearl necklace around her throat, and the black walking stick with the gold swan's head resting against her chair, Tollie and Slocum looked at her with the admiration she seemed to demand.

Mrs. English required the best of manners at the table and in her house at all times, and any infraction of table deportment was met with a slight rap on the floor with the walking stick, and a gentle but firm plea that the offender try a little harder to "be a lady." On hot summer afternoons she read aloud to the girls in the cool shade of the veranda; *Little Women*, and a series of books about a young girl who lived out west in a sod house, and *Treasure Island*. She served them endless tea parties with freshly baked raisin cookies and tart lemonade, and taught them how to arrange in sparkling crystal bowls the fragrant pink roses that bloomed in profusion on the trellis by the front steps, and on occasion she even took part in their fantasies. Tollie and Slocum had long since agreed that they would never play *The Wizard of Oz* unless Grandmother English was available to play the wicked witch and the good fairy; she played both parts with equal zeal. She could be stern, particularly when Megs got the grocery order mixed up, or served too much fried food. But during these brief scoldings, Megs simply sent her eyes up to the ceiling in an expression that seemed to say that she knew whose house this was and what would happen if she withdrew her efficient hands.

Megs was fiftyish, quite plump, and something of a challenge. She had lived in the small bedroom behind the kitchen for as long as Slocum could remember. Her face was round and smooth and always slightly pink from the heat of her kitchen, and there was a birthmark on her neck in the shape of a strawberry where her hair went into tiny fine blond curls. Her sharp blue eyes seemed always to be trained on Tollie and Slocum, scolding them for tracking up the front hall or leaving a wet towel on the bedspread.

But each night after they had gone to bed, it was Megs who tiptoed into their room, folded back their sheet, fluffed their pillows, caressed their foreheads with her smooth, strong hand, adjusted the fan on the dresser and whispered, "Dream nothing but pretty dreams, you two."

Sometimes Slocum was afraid that she loved her grandmother and Megs more than she loved her own mother. Sometimes she grew very jealous when she remembered that Tollie had been born into this heaven, was privileged to live here twelve months out of the year, and never had to return to the cold red brick house in Philadelphia. Sometimes feelings opened up inside Slocum that she couldn't understand. And sometimes, particularly this summer when she looked into the mirror, there emerged a face that was a complete stranger to her.

Generally, Tollie and Slocum played jacks on the veranda before dinner, their hair brushed and still damp from their showers, fresh in clean shorts and starched shirts, channeling all their concentration on "Around the Worlds," that most difficult of all jack tricks. On especially hot evenings, Grandmother English would join them there, holding a delicate glass of sherry in her hand, kibitzing from the porch swing, always pulling for the loser. Slocum loved these quiet intervals before dinner with the good smell of food drifting out of the screen door, and mingling with the scent of honeysuckle and roses.

But on the evening of their adventure into the Peppersalt Land, there had been no game of jacks on the veranda. And dinner was largely a silent affair with Slocum sitting on one side of her grandmother and Tollie on the other, both poking disinterestedly at Megs' gloriously browned pork chops. Slocum glanced once or twice at the two empty places farther down the table; one was for her father who would not come for another month. The other place was for her mother who had gone to Atlanta three days ago to visit old friends. A postcard had arrived yesterday addressed to Slocum with a blaze of pink azaleas on the front, and on the back a note in her mother's neat handwriting telling Slocum that she had renewed acquaintance with a lady who had been *her* girlhood chum, like Tollie and Slocum. Strange. Only now did it occur to Slocum that her mother had lied. The girlhood chum probably was not at all like Tollie. There was one major difference, and the remembrance of that difference that Tollie herself had pointed out that very afternoon in the Peppersalt Land made Slocum feel angry, and lost and very alone.

She cut off a small bite of meat, and tried to swallow it, but it got stuck in her throat. She gagged.

Across the table, Tollie giggled.

Her grandmother cautioned, "Take a sip of water, Slocum." Whereupon Slocum took a sip of water, the meat went down, and silence returned.

Everyone around the table seemed lost in thoughts as Megs moved quietly in and out of the kitchen serving vegetables and hot biscuits, none of which was devoured with any special appetite.

Finally Grandmother English stirred, straightening herself in her chair. She gave in to a brief, quick smile, then canceled it, and glanced soberly down the table. "The pig would be insulted if he could see how you two were fidgeting with his remains," she said. There was a trace of authority in her voice as if she meant to say, "All right, let's get to the bottom of this."

Slocum threw a brief glance across the table at Tollie, who was still smiling, preening herself a little at the success of something she had done, a something that she seemed determined to keep a secret.

Still no one spoke, except Grandmother English whose general expression now suggested energy and nobility and a trace of curiosity. "My father always said that if you must kill the critters for food, at least do them the honor of eating heartily." She folded her long slender hands in her lap, and leaned back in her chair. "It's strange," she added after a little, "that both of you girls should have lost your appetite at precisely the same moment."

"I haven't lost anything," said Tollie, still smiling. "In fact, I'm starved."

"Then my dear child, eat with some enthusiasm. Megs works hard to prepare good food for us. We offend her when we leave full plates on the table." She let her hand rest for a moment on Tollie's; they exchanged a smile of pure warmth. Then Tollie attacked the food on her plate with real zeal, but not without first casting a triumphant look at Slocum.

Out in the kitchen, Megs dropped a pan. Slocum's heart turned over in sudden loneliness. She missed her mother. She felt as if everything she had ever known and loved was slipping away from her, and she was powerless to bring it back. Throughout this terrible feeling she heard Tollie and Grandmother English talking together, then laughing as if at some private joke.

Tollie was telling her about her visit to the Jacksons that afternoon. Slocum thought: so that's where she disappeared to after she ran out of the Peppersalt Land.

"Howard Jackson's got a whole 'nother month to stay before he has to go back to college," announced Tollie, as if it were the most important piece of news in the world.

"Oh?" said Grandmother English. "That should make Old Spent very happy."

Spent Jackson was a longtime friend of Slocum's grandmother. They had grown up together. Spent wasn't his real name, but rather a nickname given to him when he was a boy because everytime he would get halfway through a job, he would look up and say, "Ah'se spent!" Slocum had lost count of the number of times she had heard the story. She liked Spent Jackson though. Frequently he did jobs for her grandmother, clearing a place for a new compost pile, helping her in the vegetable garden behind the house. He was a kind old man who loved to make up stories out of his head, and who seemed perfectly satisfied with a world that had provided him with just barely enough of everything.

"Well, according to Mary Jackson," Tollie was saying now, "all Howard does is argue with his father."

Grandmother English raised her eyebrows in a peculiar way as she listened. "What about, for heaven sakes?"

"She didn't say, but she said that Spent wasn't

feeling very well, and asked if I could spend the night with them tonight." Without giving Grandmother English time to reply she went on, "Mary said Slocum could come too, if she wanted to." Tollie spoke as if she were about to be contradicted, although no one uttered a word. She raised her eyes, then, gradually lowering them toward her lap, began to talk with fresh animation. "Of course, there's just one extra cot, so it might be pretty crowded," she concluded.

Grandmother English was silent. She sat looking at both girls for a little while, and although Slocum didn't dare look directly at her, she detected bewilderment, sadness, and a kind of confusion in her look. In fact there had been times this summer when Slocum wasn't certain how her grandmother really felt toward Tollie, times when she seemed to love her more than anyone else in the world, and other times when she seemed to look straight through her, or around her, not seeing her, not seeing anything at all. Finally she said, "Of course you may go, Tollie. And Slocum won't mind staying here alone tonight." She cast an inquiring glance at Slocum.

Slocum did well to nod.

Tollie leaned foward. "I'll be back first thing in the morning," she said to Slocum, only a little remorsefully. "We'll do anything you want to do."

It might have been an apology, but Slocum couldn't be certain. She didn't answer, but merely smiled politely to show that she didn't really care at all when Tollie came back, or what she did.

"Pecan pie," Megs announced, coming through the kitchen door. Then, bending close over Slocum and withholding one piece of pie, she gave everyone the benefit of her supreme authority. "No dinner, no pie," she declared, as if the sight of ignored green beans and a half-eaten pork chop was more than she could bear.

"Serve her," Grandmother English said in a tone of greater authority. And when Megs started to protest, Grandmother English bore down on her words. "Perhaps Slocum is as tired of fried foods as I am," she said. "Perhaps we could have broiled or roasted meat tomorrow." And for a moment, the two women looked at each other as if they were foes of long standing.

"It's your rule I'm breaking," muttered Megs. She served the pie. "Rules is rules, I always say," she added, directing herself chiefly to Grandmother English. But Mrs. English, still displeased, answered, "Occasionally it doesn't hurt to break the best rule, Megs."

"That's a fine thing for them to be hearing," scowled Megs, bobbing her head toward the two girls. Then very quickly, she gathered the dinner plates together and retreated to the kitchen.

Slocum had the most persistent notion that there was something wrong in the house. She had never heard her grandmother make such a statement about rules, and she'd never seen Megs glare quite so openly at everyone. Even after Tollie invited her to come upstairs with her while she packed her things, Slocum knew well enough that there was something discordant in the evening, like a tune played off key.

As Tollie was going out their bedroom door, she stopped to check the locks on her overnight bag. "You won't tell the Grandmother about—what we did this afternoon, will you?"

"No."

"Do you want to go back there tomorrow?"

"No," Slocum said firmly, remembering the grinning skull.

Tollie stood by the door, as if she were unsure of what she should say or do. "Well, I guess it doesn't matter anyway. You heard what she said at dinner, about the best rules being broken." She seemed to feel rather ill at ease at that moment. But she didn't say anything else, and closed the door behind her.

Slocum stretched out on the bed with agony in her throat. She tried to remember one single night in the past when she'd slept alone, without Tollie. She couldn't. She listened to Tollie's footsteps as she went down the stairs, heard her call good night to Grandmother English who was talking on the phone in the study, heard the screen door close. She raised up on the bed and watched her go down the road toward the Jacksons.

During the next few minutes as Tollie grew smaller and smaller, Slocum realized that she had never known such despair. She thought there would never again be giggling and whispering in the bedroom, and finally, yielding to the sorrow that had been steadily building inside her, she buried her face in her pillow and prayed to God for a miracle that would bring Tollie back.

She lay there in the darkness hour after hour, and heard the house grow quiet, with no clear-cut certainty that anyone had heard her prayer, or was even listening. There was a sense of indifference in the empty bed, and the burning memory of a white skull, the wind sighing, and the echo of a voice chanting, "Nigger! Nigger!" and the image of a black arm and a white one.

She must have slept at last and when she awakened there were voices downstairs in the front hall. After a moment, they moved away, and only two were left coming up the stairs—Tollie and Grandmother English.

"I'm sorry to be such a bother," Slocum heard Tollie saying quietly. "I tried to be polite about it, but I wanted to come home."

Then Grandmother English's voice, soft and very kind. "It's all right, Tollie. Now you go on in and get to sleep."

The door opened and closed. Tollie came a little nearer to the bed and, leaning over, whispered, "You awake?"

Tears welled up in Slocum's eyes. She remembered her fervent prayer. Hearing the familiar voice, she sat up so quickly that their heads bumped together. At last they hugged each other, and clung together, thinking of nothing but their reunion.

They lay in the dark together for a long time, saying nothing; and when it seemed that everything had been said in silence, they grew drowsy and, toes touching, they fell asleep.

THREE

"TOLLIE, WAKE UP! Howard Jackson's here," whispered Slocum. She opened her eyes in the heat of midmorning and, raising up from her pillow, saw through the window a tall young man in a dazzling white shirt cross the lawn from the dirt road, his hands shoved in his pockets, taking firm steps toward the front porch.

Mary and Spent Jackson were old familiar friends of Slocum's. But their son, Howard, was an unknown quantity. Slocum had vague memories of a tall, skinny boy in faded work clothes repairing the front step. And once her grandmother had shown her a newspaper picture that had appeared in the Budding Grove newspaper of the same tall, skinny boy standing beside a model village he had constructed out of an assortment of boxes. Then somewhere in her childhood she had lost track of Howard Jackson. Now all she knew of him was what she saw as she peered down from her window at the straight young man walking buoyantly in the heat of the morning.

He came to a halt several yards short of the front porch, and stood, as if waiting. He was a dark-skinned, curly-headed man with a firm, straight nose, very full lips which didn't quite cover a slightly protruding row of white upper teeth, beautiful black eyes, and an unusually bold expression on his face. He was not smiling. But then Slocum remembered that tall skinny boy from earlier summers, and remembered that *he* never smiled. He either was completely serious or else laughed wholeheartedly, a ringing, extremely contagious laugh. Slocum was struck by his singular beauty, poised in the bright sun, looking toward the house, as if waiting for recognition.

Again, she nudged Tollie.

Out of a deep sleep, Tollie stirred, opened one eye, grumbled something about being left alone, pulled the pillow over her head, and was quiet.

"Howard's downstairs," Slocum pleaded. She sensed Howard's influence over Tollie, and used it unconsciously to draw her friend out of sleep and into the hot humid reality of a Georgia morning.

It worked. Tollie sat up, blinking, only glanced at Slocum perched by the window, then scrambled out of bed to join her there.

At the same moment, they heard Grandmother English's voice on the porch below them. "Good morning, Howard," she called lightly, as if she were genuinely pleased to see him.

"Good morning, Mrs. English." His voice was deep, and had such a serious tone to it that both girls leaned closer to the edge of the window wondering about the nature of his visit.

He removed his hands from his pockets, and stood straight as a rod. "Mary asked me to come over and see if Tollie arrived safely last night." Slocum thought it strange that he would call his mother by her first name, Mary.

"Oh, she did, Howard," replied Grandmother English. "A little sleepy, but safe. It was considerate of you to inquire."

Grandmother English moved down the steps until she could be seen in full from the bedroom window. She had a tiny black velvet ribbon around her neck; her head was a mass of soft white hair, which went well with her straight back and light silken summer-green dress. Slocum looked down on her, wishing that she had been born as beautiful as her grandmother.

She was saying something to Howard now, so low that the girls had to lean farther out of the window in order to hear.

"It's good to see you around again," she was saying, and her voice was warm and musical. "Next year is your last year, I believe. Is that right?"

Howard stared at her for a moment, as if he hadn't understood the question.

"At school, I mean," she explained. "Just one year left, or have I miscounted?"

Still Howard stared at her, now as if she had

insulted him in some way. "No," he said, very low, and his eyes were too dark to be good.

"Oh?"

"I've quit, Mrs. English."

"Good heavens, why?" She seemed very shocked by this announcement, so shocked that for a moment or two she didn't move, as if she were trying to understand the simple content of what he had said.

Howard turned away first, and studied a bird flying up into the sky as if it were the most fascinating thing in the world. "You don't really want me to go into it now, do you?" he asked, as if speaking to the bird.

"Of course I do, I . . . "

"Why? All my father tells me to do is shut up. He doesn't want to hear. Why should you?"

"Because I'm not your father," she said, as if with a sense of real indignation. "And I'm deeply interested in anyone who tells me calmly that he is in the process of throwing away his future."

"It's my future."

"Not to throw away it isn't." Her voice trembled; Slocum had never seen her so distraught. After a moment she calmed down, her voice soft as usual. "Why, you're a born architect, Howard. You've been building things since you were a child. Remember that model town."

"I was a kid."

"It was good."

"For a kid." Howard spoke in a flat final voice, as if he didn't want to discuss it any longer. In fact he said as much. "No more talk, please, Mrs. English. I'm talked out from talking to people who hear only what they want to hear. One-way conversations are a waste of breath."

But apparently Grandmother English had no intention of honoring his request. She moved down the steps; she was still saying something to him, but her voice was so low the girls couldn't hear.

Frustrated by their sudden inability to eavesdrop, they flew away from the window toward the closet, pulling shirts off the hangers, dressing as quickly as possible, one or the other checking the window every few seconds to make sure that Howard Jackson did not leave before they arrived.

Moments later they descended the stairs at breakneck speed, barely escaping a collision with Megs who was just starting up with an armload of clean linen.

"Hey, you two," she called after them, but to no avail.

They stopped just inside the screen door, long enough to catch their breath and straighten themselves, then went out onto the porch, serene and ladylike.

Grandmother English was sitting on the porch swing, pushing gently at the floor with her walking stick, a confused but almost detached expression on her face. "It's not always easy, Howard," she was saying.

"It's not a matter of things being easy, Mrs. English," Howard replied. He leaned against the hand railing near the bottom of the step, his eyes down, a sober cast to his face. "This time next year I would have been a full-fledged architect with five years of training and no job."

"You don't know that for a certainty."

"Oh?" Howard took the small word up the scale

and left it there. He smiled in a way that had nothing to do with humor.

Grandmother English went on. "You see, Howard—"

"Oh, I see very well, Mrs. English," he interrupted. "There's nothing wrong with my eyesight, nothing at all. For example, I can look at a slum and see new apartments and homes. I can look at an empty field and see a park and playgrounds. Then I can look at the face of the man who owns that slum or that field, and I can see that he has a white face. And I can look at the man behind the desk in the bank and see that his face is white, too. And all I have to do is look in the mirror to know that this time next year, I would have been an unemployed architect." Again he laughed, a choked sound. "Old Spent says I should come home and raise corn and cotton with him."

Slocum could tell that her grandmother was listening very carefully to Howard's words. She sat perfectly still in the swing and rubbed the golden swan's head on her walking stick, her eyes clouded. She appeared to be deep in thought. "So what are you going to do?" she asked.

Howard studied the palms of his hands. "I think I'll go back North. There's lots happening there."

Grandmother English stared at him for a long time. Something, anger, resignation crossed her face. She looked very displeased, as if she were sorry the morning had ever come at all. Finally she drew a deep breath. "I know you well enough to know that you'll do very well, Howard, no matter what happens," she said weakly.

Howard answered her immediately. "I have every

intention of doing better than very well," he said. "No matter what happens!"

Then Grandmother English said nothing more; she looked as if she were more displeased with herself than she was with Howard.

Having overheard the tag end of a conversation they didn't understand, both girls stopped close to the door. Perhaps it was because her grandmother was frowning and Howard's face had a haughty expression, or because Tollie went directly to Howard's side and left her standing alone and embarrassed, but Slocum suddenly experienced as much fear as curiosity for the young man.

Everyone said good morning to everyone else, and Slocum went to sit beside her grandmother in the swing. Her fear did not become a reality however, until Howard moved one step closer to the porch and spoke directly to her. "Mary said that she thought you two would enjoy going fishing at Hunter's Lake today," he said, and there was something in the way he said it that made Slocum think it was more Mary's idea than his own.

Tollie squealed and jumped up from the bottom step where she had crouched, gazing adoringly at Howard. Slocum only blushed and couldn't say a word. Howard had a habit of fixing his eyes without blinking on the person to whom he was speaking, so that no matter how friendly and kind he appeared to be, his face, his eyes always seemed to indicate something else.

Slocum's grandmother nudged her into good manners. "Say something, Slocum, or are you still asleep?"

"Yes, thank you," Slocum replied. "I'd like that

very much."

"They both would enjoy it," confirmed Grandmother English. "They've been after Megs to take them all summer. But I'm afraid Megs is getting old and sedentary."

"And cowardly?" Howard added this under his breath, almost as if he hoped that no one would hear.

But Grandmother English heard. "That's enough," she said, and her voice was as stern and harsh as Slocum had ever heard it.

For a moment Howard looked as if it wasn't enough at all. But apparently he changed his mind about saying anything else on the subject. "Then I'll go get the truck and pick you up in ten minutes," he said to Tollie. He ruffled her hair, fixing her with his penetrating eyes. "Get moving, black girl," he teased, his voice low. "We're going fishing. Ain't that what we'se suppose to do best?" As Howard imitated a deep southern drawl, Slocum looked up. He sounded just like Old Spent for a moment.

Tollie giggled and ducked her chin. Anyone could see that she particularly prized her friendship with Howard. She watched him straighten his unusually muscular shoulders, and waved at him three times as she was leaving the porch.

From inside the screen door, Megs called the girls for toast and eggs. Tollie rushed in as always, claiming she was starved. Slocum followed less quickly, stopping inside the door to hear the tag end of the conversation on the porch.

Howard had started walking toward the road, when suddenly he stopped and turned back. "Don't get me wrong," he said. "I appreciate your helping Old Spent to help me."

Grandmother English started to protest, but Howard never gave her a chance. "I've known for a long time that Old Spent's savings came mostly from your bank account."

She looked very embarrassed and kept her eyes down. "What difference does it make where the money came from?" she asked quietly.

"It makes a lot of difference to me," he replied. Sorry you can't understand why. But the point is, I don't want or need your help anymore. I don't need anyone's help."

Now she looked up. "Are you sure of that?"

"More sure than I've ever been of anything in my life." They stared at each other for a moment longer, then Howard turned without a word, and started off toward the road.

Slocum stood in the shadows of the doorway, looking at her grandmother who still sat in the swing, no longer pushing gently on the floor with her walking stick, but instead gazing out at the empty space where Howard had stood, a worried, lost, bewildered look in her eyes.

A short time later, the girls were settled comfortably in the front seat of Howard Jackson's pickup truck, Tollie sitting in the middle, Slocum by the window, and Howard driving effortlessly down the road that was pitted with shallow gulleys and bordered on both sides by brilliant yellow patches of black-eyed Susans.

In her lap, Slocum cradled a glass jar of beef broth, prepared by her grandmother with instructions to drop it off at Mary Jackson's for Old Spent. According to Slocum's grandmother, there were few ailments that plagued the human body that could not be cured with one steaming cup of rich brown beef broth. The jar was still warm against her hands, and it was as if the pungent odor of roasting beef had followed the girls out of Megs' kitchen and into Howard's truck, confirming the fact that there would not be fried food on the dinner table that night. Everything was delightful, with Tollie sitting primly, hands folded on her bare legs, obviously determined to impress Howard with her dignity and help him forget her scant twelve years. Through the narrow window behind her, Slocum saw the fishing poles joggling with each bump in the road and the battered minnow can sliding back and forth. It was going to be a glorious day except for that small gloomy memory of Grandmother English's eyes.

At the sight of the small white frame house sitting on the left hand side of the road, Howard broke speed and brought the truck to a rattling stop, causing a cloud of pink dust to rise up off the red clay road.

"Go do what you have to do," he said, bending over to wipe his forehead on the sleeve of his shirt, never taking his hands off the steering wheel. Slocum waited for a moment to see if he would turn off the ignition, and in that moment, Howard tightened his grip on the wheel and, in a voice which clearly showed that he was uncomfortably hot, said again, "Well, go on. What are you waiting for?"

Both girls scurried out of the truck door with such haste that Slocum stumbled and almost dropped the jar of beef broth. Tollie caught her elbow, and although not a word was spoken, Slocum wondered if perhaps Tollie didn't share her same feelings of mingled fear and anxiety.

The house seemed extraordinarily quiet; the front door was standing wide open, and a hoe had been left carelessly on the walk. Slocum carried the beef broth as steadily as possible. Walking close beside her was Tollie who, acting on instructions from Grandmother English, planned to apologize to Mary Jackson for leaving so abruptly the night before.

When they stood a few feet from the opened door, Slocum called out, "Mrs. Jackson?" Bright-colored zinnias bloomed in profusion around the small neat white house, and bees buzzed in a honeysuckle vine at one end of the porch. Up close, Slocum noticed that the house had a faint pink tinge caused by layers of dust that had blown on it from the road.

Out of the darkness of the room, Mary Jackson appeared, plump and round and rather shapeless in her faded dress, and a few lines of glistening white in her dark hair. Her shoulders were bent, and the dark skin on her forehead was creased with wrinkles. Although she looked directly at the girls, she seemed not to see them. In her hand was a wet white cloth dripping water. "It's Old Spent," she said, in a barely audible voice. "Sun beat him down."

She seemed so terribly worried; she glanced beyond the girls toward the truck waiting at the edge of the road. Then a smile broke through the concern on her face and she said something about forgetting her manners, and urged the girls to come inside where it was cool.

Blinded by the sun, at first Slocum saw nothing. Then things gradually came into view; directly across the room a small couch where Spent Jackson was resting, in the middle a round table covered with a blue and white checkered oil cloth with a small bouquet of zinnias in a dark green jar, several chairs of various sizes and descriptions, and on the wall two calendar pictures, one of puppies on a clipped green lawn and the other a Christmas dinner with a roasted turkey on a heavily laden table. Above the calendars was a large picture of Christ with a bleeding forehead. Slocum knew the room well, having spent many happy hours there listening to Spent Jackson tell stories. Now to see the old man lying so still on the couch alarmed her.

In some confusion, she tried to explain why they had come, and placed the glass jar of beef broth on the table, and asked Mary Jackson if she wanted her to get her grandmother.

"No," said Mrs. Jackson with a smile, gently placing the wet cloth on the old man's forehead. "He'll be all right." Then, after a brief pause: "The sun told him what I've been telling him for years, that he passed sixteen a long time ago."

"Pshaw!" said a deep but weak voice from beneath the damp cloth.

Just then a horn sounded out in the road and, feeling quite certain that Howard was losing even more patience, both girls inched toward the door.

"You two run along," Mary said, moving a fan back and forth in front of Spent's face. Her lips were closed, and her eyes had such a serious cast that Slocum wasn't certain whether they should leave or not. But again Mary reassured them that everything was going to be all right, and told Slocum to be sure and thank her grandmother for the broth, and even walked with them to the door and, with fresh animation in her voice, told them to catch only the biggest fish.

At the door, Mary Jackson suddenly fell silent and again became thoughtful. She gazed out across the shimmering heat at the waiting truck and Howard.

"Do you want me to call him for you?" asked Tollie.

"No, just tell him to drive like he had good sense." And with that she turned and went back into the house.

Inside the truck, the girls, both talking at once, told Howard about his father. The young man listened intently; once his hand moved down toward the key in the ignition, as if he meant to turn it off. He looked toward the small white house, his head bent forward between his shoulders. Then suddenly he rammed the gear shift to the floor, causing the truck to leap forward in a burst of speed. Tollie gripped the dashboard for balance, while Slocum looked at Howard in silence and wondered at the sad, grown-up expression which she had noticed on his strong, glistening face, and she remembered that the tall, skinny boy who used to repair the front steps and build model villages had a sad, grown-up expression in his face, too.

There was a blur of yellow and green outside the truck window. On one side of the road a vast field of parched grain, intersected here and there by shallow gullies, glimmered with dry heat and stretched away like a worn carpet clear to the horizon; on the other side several men worked with hoes down long rows of corn without a rustle of wind to cool them. Slocum brooded on the scene outside the window, heedless of the fact that huge drops of sweat were running down the side of her face and that her shirt was wet against her back. She rested her head against the closed window, heavyhearted and resentful that the sun would hurt someone who was as gentle and good as Spent Jackson.

"Air!" cried Tollie, melodramatically, reaching across Slocum to roll down the window.

Howard, his head still bowed, was thoughtfully watching first the dusty road running away under the wheels, then the men working in the fields. He maintained his usual silence for several moments, although Slocum was not foolish enough to believe that his mind was empty. In a way she felt sorry for him, and would have liked to have said something, but she could only think of the most casual remarks that made no sense, and did not seem to fit in with the events of the morning.

Then suddenly, and very softly, Howard began speaking, as if for his own comfort and enjoyment, a poem of sorts, words at first unintelligible, his eyes still trained on the men working in the fields:

> Bowed by the weight of centuries,
> He leans upon his hoe, and
>   gazes on the ground,
> The emptiness of ages in his face,
> And on his back the burden of the world.

His voice drifted off, taking the rest of the words with it, leaving a lovely echo that could be heard above the rattle of the truck.

Tollie blinked and looked up. "He learned that at college," she grinned, pridefully, as if she'd had something to do with it.

"I did not," Howard said, sternly. Then in a curious, softer afterthought, he added, "I learned it a long time ago—from that tired old man back there."

Gently he jerked his head over his shoulder in the direction of the small white frame house which had now disappeared from view over a rise of land.

"Say some more," Tollie begged. "Please say the rest of it."

Briefly Howard glanced up toward the roof of the truck. Leaning nonchalantly against the door, pleasure spread all over his face. "I'm not sure I can remember the rest," he said. "Let's see—" His eyes wrinkled and disappeared behind slightly closed lids. "It goes something like this:

> How will it be with kingdoms
>   and with kings—
> With those who shaped him to
>   the thing he is—
> When this dumb terror shall rise
>   to judge the world,
> After the silence of the centuries?"

His voice, a deep baritone, made music out of the words. Slocum felt the skin crawl at the back of her neck.

Tollie was equally impressed. "Old Spent taught you that?" she asked.

"He did," Howard replied. "He's been reading white man's poems for as long as I can remember, and spouting them off like they were gospel."

Both girls caught the special word. Slocum elected to let it pass without discussion, but not Tollie. She gazed at him worshipfully. "Say a black man's poem, Howard. Do you know any?"

For just a moment a flicker of a smile creased the young man's stern face. "Know plenty," he said, "but I don't think they're fit for your ears."

"Oh say one, say one," chanted Tollie. "Say one for Slocum."

"I doubt if Slocum could care less whether I said anything or not." He looked out at the shimmering fields, his dark eyes shining with what appeared to be a deep and nameless sorrow. "I tell you what," he said, "I'll sing you a black man's song. How will that be?" He looked away for a moment, and it was while his face was turned away that his voice came out in song, a slow mournful dirge with words to match, solemn, measured and sorrowful:

I walk through the churchyard to lay
  this body down;
I know moon-rise, I know star-rise;
I walk in the moonlight, I walk in the starlight;
I'll lie in the grave and stretch out my arms,
I'll go to judgment in the evening of the day,
And my soul and thy soul shall meet that day,
When I lay this body down.

When the song was over the air within the truck lay silent. There was not a whisper of wind from the cloudless sky.

Howard coughed as if embarrassed. "That's a black man's song, Tollie," and then he said no more, but seemed to slump behind the wheel and gaze, unseeing at the distant ridge of pines all bathed in sunlight.

Slocum watched him as he went off into his own thoughts. She had been deeply impressed by the song, by everything that Howard had said. The feeling was not new to her, but it was difficult to explain, the sensation of her skin crawling, and goose-bumps causing the hair on her arm to stand up, and a heavy stinging behind her eyes. She felt like this when she said the "Pledge of Allegiance" with her classmates in school, when she concentrated on the words of the "Star Spangled Banner" instead of the difficult melody, when she recited "The Lord's Prayer" in church, when she sang "We Gather Together" at Thanksgiving, and "Silent Night" at Christmastime, and on every occasion that called for small, insignificant words that were strung together in a large, significant manner—sensations that left her more with a feeling than with a knowing. Now as she stole a glance sidewards at Howard's face, his expression seemed to mirror an ache and longing she had so often felt when the beauty of the world was too intense, when the need to hold and keep a day, an hour, a minute left her with a sense of indescribable sorrow.

Finally she spoke, the need to express herself strong within her. "The song was beautiful, Howard. I guess it isn't important who made it up."

Tollie started in surprise, and turned a shocked face in Slocum's direction. "You just think it isn't important," she said with a high and mighty air.

Slocum felt her own face flush angrily. She started to say something sharp, but then she noticed that Tollie had looked to Howard to settle the matter. Both girls waited dimly, faltering a little under the weight of an argument they just barely understood.

"Howard?" Tollie urged. "It *is* important, isn't it?"

He looked up, and after a moment, spoke with some effort. "I used to think it wasn't important. Old Spent says it isn't. But Old Spent and I don't agree on much of anything anymore."

Bewildered, Slocum said, "He's your father . . . "

"So?"

Tollie joined Howard's side. "Honestly, Slocum, sometimes you say the dumbest things. Fathers aren't always right."

There was something in Tollie's attitude, in the accusation of being dumb that infuriated Slocum. She wanted very much to retaliate, to ask Tollie how it was that she knew so much about fathers when she didn't even have one. But she kept quiet and wished that she hadn't come with them today, wished that she was back at Grandmother English's house, that her mother was home from Atlanta. She thought too for just an instant how simple it would be if everyone were the same color.

Howard seemed to sense her confusion. He glanced over at her, his face stern. "Maybe Slocum is right," he said. "Maybe it wasn't important who wrote the song. Whoever wrote it is dead now, so let's just drop the subject." His voice was cold, almost angry.

Tollie ducked her head, and with some difficulty kept quiet. Across the expanse of the truck, Slocum and Howard exchanged a curious look. Slocum was certain that he was angry with her, although she wasn't certain why. She had merely voiced an opinion, and her opinion was as valid as his.

She burrowed down into the worn seat of the old truck and tried to breathe deeply. Absolutely nothing had been accomplished by the discussion. She wished that she could tell Tollie how sorry she was that they had argued. She decided that she would tell Tollie that night that from now on they both should stay away from dangerous subjects that could lead to fights.

The crossroads appeared through the front windshield. The sun was high in the sky. Cicero's store sat in a mirage of heat waves.

"I could use something cold to drink," Howard said, obviously trying to change the mood inside the truck.

Tollie and Slocum seconded the motion with less than wholehearted enthusiasm. Slocum had the feeling that the day had been ruined. Whatever had happened inside the truck had left a tension that seemed to war with the prospect of a festive fishing trip.

Howard brought the truck to a quick stop in front of Cicero's store. On the way up the steps, he put his hand on Slocum's head and ruffled her hair in the same manner that earlier that morning he had ruffled Tollie's.

Slocum tried to thank him for the gesture, without words, but by merely giggling as Tollie had done.

Then he led the girls up the steps and into the cool dark shadows of Cicero's store.

FOUR

Mr. Cicero did not move from behind his cash register. "G'morning, people," he said to the three who came in, shifting slightly on his stool.

He was a short, round man of about fifty with a serene, sleepy expression on his face. Over his shirt and trousers he wore a soiled white butcher's apron with large pockets and tattered ties that drooped down his back. Even though the only hair he had left was a sparse semicircular fringe on the back of his head and the set of his upper lip plainly showed a deficiency of teeth, his face was still remarkably young and strong looking.

Cicero had owned this store for as long as anyone could remember. It was a long concrete block building decorated with chipping green paint and an assortment of faded political posters and signs announcing the arrival of Barnum and Bailey Circus and the pleasures of Coca Cola. Inside the store the aisles were dark and dingy and cluttered with unpacked cartons of canned goods. The air was a fragrant blend of spice and dill pickles and freshly ground coffee. It was isolated and lonely at the crossroads, and the store was much smaller and not nearly as well stocked as the big supermarkets in Budding Grove. People wondered how old Cicero managed to stay in business with so much competition from the big stores in town. No one was ever quite sure, although it was generally believed that Cicero had sought out a place where he could escape his wife's sharp tongue. Slocum's grandmother had her own idea which she had on occasion confided to Megs, and Slocum had overheard. "Sometimes I think old Cicero runs that store down there so he can overcharge the farmers, both black and white. His prices are exorbitant."

Whatever the reason, Cicero ran his store and made a profit. Within moments after Howard and the girls had entered the door, the expression on Cicero's face changed from one of sleepy-eyed lethargy to close scrutiny. He was wary of shoplifters; sometimes barefoot, skinny children would wander in with their parents, and fill the insides of their loose-hanging overalls with more merchandise than the parents had purchased. Last summer Megs had gossiped for days when Cicero had pressed charges against a white tenant family, and had wrung her hands and fretted because she said the "criminals" were good people. She announced that Cicero would have his own mother arrested if she disturbed so much as the dust on his counter.

Remembering all this, Slocum's shyness increased, and having caught the sound of the bell jangling furiously as they opened the door, she thought it best to withdraw and let Howard transact their small business. Down the long center aisle, Tollie went skipping toward the cooler where the soda pop was stored. Howard exchanged only the briefest nod with Cicero and followed after Tollie toward the cooler. Slocum studied Cicero as he stood awkwardly behind the counter. She noticed for the first time the sallow cast of his face, and the deep-set eyes with dark shadows under them, and hands and arms that were immense for a man of his stature. He had a harsh, unpleasant expression, but he seemed to be very satisfied with himself and was, in Slocum's opinion, exactly the way a man who has a wife with a sharp tongue, and makes a profit, would be.

He stood watching Tollie and Howard for some time without saying a word; then he glanced in the opposite direction toward Slocum and looked as if he meant to speak, but after glancing once more toward the rear of his store where Howard and Tollie were gathering cold drinks and small bags of potato chips, he somehow changed his mind. When Howard had collected all of the items and placed them on the counter, Cicero asked, as if to make conversation, if it was "hot enough for everybody."

"Too hot," Howard replied lightly. "Slocum, you and Tollie open these bottles back there, and we'll pay the deposit and take them with us."

Slocum went to do as she was told. As she passed by the counter, she heard Mr. Cicero say, "Cokes is fine, Jackson, but not that!" and his voice sounded low when he said it.

On the counter, close to the assortment of potato chips and candy bars there were two cans of beer, still cold and dripping from the cooler. "You see," Cicero went on, nonchalantly, "it ain't never too smart in my books for a man to be drinking when he's toting around a bunch of children. So the beer is out, but you're welcome to this stuff," he added with an expressive gesture, moving the beer cans to one side.

"Sir?" said Howard, stepping closer to the counter, as if he hadn't heard what the man had said.

"No beer!" Cicero said again, and this time there was no margin in his voice. "That back there is Mrs. English's granddaughter, and if you think for a minute, I'm going to allow . . . "

"Tollie's back there, too," said Howard quizzically, as if trying hard to understand what all the fuss was about.

"That's my point, my very point," snapped Cicero, "and don't go questioning me about what I allow in my store, because what I allow in my store had damn well better be my own business. You hear? Now pay for the rest of that stuff, and let's go back to talking about the weather."

Howard, who looked like a stern and respectable younger version of his father, seemed to want to do exactly what Cicero suggested. From the way his hand fiddled with the loose change in his pocket, it looked as if he would pay for the items and let the matter drop. But then a quite different expression crossed his face; he moved still closer to the counter and looked disapprovingly at Cicero.

"I would like those two cans of beer," he said, avoiding further explanations. "I'll pay whatever they cost."

It was more the silence than the sound of the men's voices raised in dispute that alarmed Slocum and Tollie. They moved carefully away from the cooler toward the front door of the store, awed and uncertain about what they should do. "Let's go," Tollie whispered to Howard as they passed by.

"The kid's got more sense than you have, Jackson," grinned Cicero, revealing gaps between his teeth.

"I want that beer," Howard repeated, measuring out each word.

"Well, now, I'd say that's just about the main trouble with you people," said Cicero. "You been getting just about too much of everything you want."

"Do you make it a habit of telling your customers what to buy?"

"When I think it's for their own good, and when they don't use good judgment in making their own decisions," snapped Cicero, his eyes sullen.

"Do you think you're qualified to serve as judge and jury for the entire human race?"

Suddenly Cicero flew into a rage, his voice and face contorted by anger. "Now I'm telling you for the last time, Jackson, ain't no one got a right to come into my store and force me to sell them one damn thing. You hear? You ain't up North now, so you just get that through your head. Things move slower down here, a lot slower. Now you get them items off the counter, give me the correct change, then clear out of here, and if I was you I'd take Mrs. English's granddaughter back where she belongs, and stop messing around with folks who is respected in these parts."

Deeply distressed by all they were hearing, the two girls inched close to the front door. Slocum felt as if she should tell Mr. Cicero that she was with Howard because she wanted to be with him. But when she tried to open her mouth, the words stuck in her throat. And Tollie was there, gripping her hand so hard that her fingers were turning numb.

Apparently neither man noticed the girls' discomfiture, but continued to glare at each other as if they were seeing each other for the first time. If it had not been for the seriousness of the situation, Slocum would have laughed at the way they were standing in identical positions, both grasping the edge of the counter.

Howard was breathing hard, his voice harsh with dislike. "Old man, you're wrong," he said, quietly.

Cicero ran his hand across his forehead, then reached for the broom behind him. "Look at who's talking," he said, his voice barely a whisper. "I know scum when I see it, and I'm looking at it right now. And you want me to show you what I do when I find scum on the floor of my store?" And all the time he was talking, he was moving slowly out from behind the counter, easing the broom up into the air until he was grasping it by the bristles, holding it as though he were about to bat a ball.

Slocum felt sick. It had all happened so fast; one minute they were talking and singing in the truck, and the next minute the two men were here in Cicero's store, glaring at each other as if there were nothing but hate in their hearts. She felt that if Howard didn't leave soon, Cicero was going to hit him. She watched his face to see if there was any indication that he was ready to leave.

But there was nothing in Howard's face that day that spoke of retreat. He stood there, silent before the approaching Cicero, his back straight, his hands clenched at his sides.

Finally he said, "If you think you're going to accomplish anything by using that—"

Suddenly Cicero swung the broomstick directly at Howard's head. Tollie screamed shrilly. Something seemed to rise higher and higher inside Slocum and began to constrict her chest and choke her; her eyes filled with tears and she could only barely make out the two men grappling for possession of the broom.

Howard emerged victorious. He hurled the broom halfway down the long center aisle. "I had no intention of quarreling with you," he gasped, giving Cicero a slight push.

"Get out!"

Howard took Cicero by the arm as if he were about to lead him someplace; he drew back his fist, and struck him such a blow that Cicero flew backwards into an arrangement of canned peaches. Above the clatter of cans and the groan that issued from Cicero's lips, both girls screamed as they watched the man slump to the floor, his eyes closed, blood rushing from his mouth.

For a long moment, no one spoke, but all three stood staring down at the unconscious Cicero, as if they were afraid to move. Howard went to the door and looked the girls full in the face.

"I'm sorry," he said in a most ordinary voice, without a trace of anger. "Don't be frightened. I'm—sorry."

He held out his hands.

"Did you hear me? I said I was sorry." Suddenly he enclosed both girls in his arms, pressing them close to his side.

Slocum looked up at him, as if it wasn't difficult at all to make out why he had tears in his eyes. She felt more sad than frightened. It was then that she realized for the first time that she—that is her family, her grandmother, Tollie—were not the only people in the world, but that there existed another life, that of people who had nothing in common with each other, cared nothing about each other, and didn't even have an idea or care that the other existed. No doubt she knew all that before, but not the way she got to know it now, watching Howard's face contort with remorse, glancing at the still Cicero on the floor.

Then there was Howard again urging them toward the truck and the hot sun outside, and Tollie whimpering, "Oh Lord, Lord," over and over again.

And Slocum suddenly became aware that her view of things was completely changing, as though all the objects she had been seeing up till then all at once had turned a new, unfamiliar side to her.

FIVE

HOWARD DROVE the truck back down the road in the same direction from which they had come. In the back the fishing poles and minnow can rattled together disconsolately. The idea that it was necessary for Howard to run away became a conviction only after a brief discussion, because it was an entirely different idea from the one that Tollie and Slocum shared. The fight in the store had deeply affected the girls, and they felt that all three of them should go to Grandmother English and relate the incident in full.

"She'll know what to do, Howard," Slocum said, quite casually, hoping to conceal her fear.

He didn't blink an eye, although he seemed to be confused. "I don't know," he said. "I'm not sure. That's why I want you two to go to her and tell her exactly what happened."

"But why don't you come with us?" asked Tollie.

"Because I can't," replied Howard, and from the set of his lips, it looked as if he had resolved never to answer another question as long as he lived.

He stopped the truck within sight of his parents' home. Both girls looked at him, seeing the terrible expression on his face. It had suddenly become cold, severe. He turned off the ignition, and let his hand drop limply. If he had been angry or resentful, it might have been easier on all of them. But he didn't scold, or say a harsh word about Cicero or anyone; he just shook his head as he stared toward the distant green fringe of the Peppersalt Land.

"Somehow I can't quite remember how it all happened now." He smiled apologetically. Slocum tried to remember the events leading up to the actual blows, imagining how she would tell the story to her grandmother. She, too, had trouble remembering the exact cause and the words that had been exchanged. "Howard?" she asked in a small voice. "I'm not certain I know exactly what to tell Grandmother."

He looked at her absently for a moment, and then nodded. "I know you'll tell her the right thing. And you, too, Tollie. I need both of you. And don't worry about me." He got out of the truck and straightened his shirt inside his belt. "I think I'll just take a long walk," he smiled. "See you around."

He bobbed his head toward the girls, and told

them once again to go straight home. Then he started off in long strides across the open field, his arms swinging easily at his side. He did not look back; he did not even show by so much as a single glance that he was heading straight in the direction of the Peppersalt Land.

Tollie uttered an amazed, "Oh-h-h" when it became clear to her where Howard was going. She glanced at Slocum, then looked fearfully away toward the dark green trees behind which there were quicksand bogs and poisonous snakes and human skulls.

"Come on," said Slocum. "We have to tell Grandmother—something. Howard said he needed us, and after all, we were there." Again she sounded a brave note in the hot heavy silence of the truck, and hoped that Tollie didn't notice how false it was.

What had started out to be a glorious morning ended in empty feelings of fear and anger, too terrible even to talk about. Cicero had been wrong, but then Howard had been wrong too in a way. And what was to be gained by running off into the Peppersalt Land where a wrong step could be fatal, and where the vines were thick enough and strong enough to hang a man?

Slocum shook her head and tried to clear the fear and confusion. They left the truck and walked quickly past the Jackson house, hoping, praying that no one would call to them, forgetting for the moment old Spent's bout with the sun. Tollie, in a fit of nervous energy, kept running a little ahead of Slocum, calling back for her to "Hurry!" But as far as Slocum was concerned, there was no need for haste. They would arrive soon enough and would have to spill out the dreadful story, and no matter how hard she tried to imagine exactly what she would say, no words came to her mind that made sense. She remembered her grandmother's conversation with Howard earlier that morning, and she wondered if she could even begin to convince her that Howard was not to blame.

The sun climbed high in the sky to a noon position and cast light on a dense white cloud that covered the far horizon, and all about Slocum the countryside was bathed in a blindingly brilliant radiance. The road ahead stretched like a wide tattered brown ribbon between fields of dry stubble. Here and there they passed beneath a tree by the road, or a young sapling with small sticky leaves, casting a motionless shadow on the clay ruts and short green weeds. The monotonous noise of their footsteps and the hum of locusts did not drown the echo of the song which Howard had sung for them in the truck. Slocum still could hear "Thy Soul and My Soul" inside her head. And the smell of sweat and dust was overpowered by the spicy fragrance of Cicero's store, and the echo of men's voices raised in anger. Slocum felt a deep, despairing unrest, a longing to do and say something, and the realization that her head was empty of thought and action.

Grandmother English came down the stairs, wearing the rose-colored dress that she wore into town and carrying a stack of white envelopes with little see-through windows which meant, Slocum supposed, that she was going to pay the household bills. When she had seated herself in an armchair close to the coffee table, she drew a long breath, and began stacking the envelopes into some kind of order.

"I see the fishing trip is off," she said quietly. "I

didn't realize how late it was. It's almost lunchtime. I'm very hungry."

The girls sat close to each other on the sofa. The suggestion that it was almost lunch time meant less than nothing to them. Slocum cleared her throat and began shakily. "Something happened at—"

Then Grandmother English did an amazing thing. She called Megs and asked if it would be possible to serve sandwiches in the living room. Eating in the gold and green velvet living room was strictly forbidden, as forbidden as coming to the dinner table with dirty finger nails, or going into the Peppersalt Land.

When the matter of lunch had been settled, she leaned back in the armchair, relaxed and perfectly at ease. "Did you deliver the beef broth to Mary Jackson? How is Old Spent? I understand that he had some difficulty with the sun. But then he's strong, one of the strongest persons I've ever known."

Slocum felt that for some reason her grandmother did not want to hear about the events of the morning. And how did she know about Spent Jackson? She moved closer to Tollie, feeling very wretched and awkward, trying not to think about the food that she would shortly be called upon to eat.

Megs brought the sandwiches on a tray with a tall dripping pitcher of fruit punch. She said nothing but kept her eyes down, as if a sort of invisible barrier were around her. This behavior was most unlike Megs, who always had to know everything about everything.

Grandmother English took her time over a little triangle of bread, chewing each bit agonizingly slowly, and helping herself to a second one, and then a glass of fruit punch. When she had finally finished, she wiped her fingers carefully on the napkin, and then, settling back into the armchair, she began sorting through the stack of envelopes again.

"You were about to tell me something that happened at Cicero's this morning, Slocum," she said, not even looking at the girls, but still concentrating on the envelopes in her lap.

Tollie nudged Slocum, who was still fingering a half-eaten pimento cheese sandwich. The cheese tasted like chalk. She returned the sandwich to the platter, and wondered vaguely why Tollie had nudged her. *She* had been there. Why couldn't *she* tell the story, or at least start it? But then she saw in her mind's eye the image of Cicero slumped on the floor bleeding from the mouth. She felt the weight of Howard's arm as he had pressed the girls close, the detailed look of sorrow in his eyes, heard the echo of his song "Thy Soul and My Soul." And she sat as straight as she could, and tried to clear her head, so that she would, at least for once in her life, make sense.

The story came hard. As she tried to remember the words that the two men had exchanged, her grandmother seemed to lose interest, and stared at the rose pattern in the carpet. Once it seemed to Slocum that her voice was climbing higher and higher so that she heard herself as nothing more than a shrill, piping child. But she did not feel like a child. She felt old, very old, and for some reason, she fixed her eyes on a point outside the window, on the footpath that stretched across the side lawn toward the back fence, then disappeared behind the window, going in the direction of the terrible, ominous Peppersalt Land.

Then it was over, and Grandmother English dropped her hands into her lap. Slocum was too exhausted to say anything more even though she realized that she had stopped short of the true end of the story. She had simply said that they got back into the truck and left.

"Disgraceful, if you ask me," murmured Megs, who had stood silently at the door listening to the entire recital.

Grandmother English looked up at the sound of her voice, and she tried to take a deep breath of air, but something got clogged in her throat and she gave a little cough, covering her mouth with her hand and holding it there long after the cough had died. Slocum remembered what her grandmother had told her when she was a little girl, that people always cover their mouths with their hands when they cough so their souls wouldn't fly out.

"Thank you for telling me about it, Slocum," she said. "Although I must confess that Cicero phoned me only a few moments before you girls came in."

Slocum said nothing. She was relieved that Cicero wasn't dead, and was at least well enough to use the telephone. But she was very angry that her grandmother had known all along, and still insisted on hearing the difficult story again.

"Only I'm afraid," her grandmother continued quietly, "that we haven't heard the end of it. Where is Howard now?"

At last Tollie found her voice. "Howard's not to blame," she declared.

"I said nothing about blame, Tollie." Grandmother English hesitated. "Besides it's too large a word to consider now," and she looked grateful that she did not have to consider it at all. "Where is Howard?" she asked again.

Slocum roused to a quick fury. "It was Cicero who started it all," she pleaded. "He said such terrible things."

"Your grandmother didn't ask you who started it," snapped Megs. "She just wants to know—"

"Well, isn't it important who started it?" cried Slocum. "Tollie's right. Howard tried to stop it." She hesitated, realizing that this wasn't exactly the truth. She frowned at Megs. "If Cicero had treated you like he treated Howard, you probably would have hit him, too."

Megs did not respond immediately to this. Her smile was mournful but very kind. "I've been wanting to give Cicero a piece of my mind for years now, Slocum, and I probably will someday. But not in the way Howard did it."

"Well, I know one thing," muttered Slocum. "I'll never set foot in that store again. Never!"

"Me either," echoed Tollie.

Grandmother English studied the girls closely. "If you could tell me where Howard is at this moment, you both would be helping matters a great deal. Whether any of us go back into the store is unimportant." She leaned forward and made a direct plea. "Tollie, Slocum, what happened this morning may have been very one-sided and unjust, but let's not add to the injustice with more deceit. I'm not blaming anyone." Her expression was confused, her brow furrowed. "I'm not certain I'd know who to blame anyway." Again her voice broke; she looked around at the space about her, as if searching for something. "I just want to know where Howard is now. Where did he go?"

They sat in silence after that, and listened to the sounds of glasses rattling together as Megs cleared away the lunch tray. Grandmother English's words weighed down on both girls; they knew that she had expressed something that was very true, but they both felt as well that she had left out something that was equally true. And Slocum knew all too well the expression on her grandmother's face; she'd seen it earlier that morning with Howard on the porch, bewilderment and fatigue, as if she were faced again with an everlasting and insoluble problem.

"Do you know where Howard is now?" she asked again softly. "Or at least do you know where he was going?"

Slocum and Tollie glanced at each other, then looked down and said nothing.

Megs brushed crumbs off the coffee table into her hand. "What I know about Howard," she said, "is enough to tell me that he has a good head on his shoulders. He doesn't need the protection of two girls."

This was not true. Slocum remembered what Howard had said to them. "I need your help now. I know I can count on you."

Just then the telephone rang; its ring sounded shrill and sudden, causing Slocum's heart to stop. Megs answered it, then quietly handed it to Grandmother English. All she said was "Yes" three times, and ran her fingers across her forehead. She was quite calm and matter-of-fact when she put down the receiver and handed the phone back to Megs.

"That was Cicero," she said. "He asked if you had arrived home safely, and if you had told me what had happened. He wants to come by for a moment with the sheriff."

Tollie sank down into the sofa and muttered, "Oh, Lord," just as she had done after Howard had hit Cicero.

"Of course you realize that they will ask questions," said Grandmother English.

"I know," replied Slocum, returning her grandmother's gaze.

"And you will tell them everything you know?"

Slocum hesitated. "I'll tell them exactly what I told you," she said.

For an instant a cold severe expression crossed her grandmother's face. She restacked the envelopes in her lap with a flash of energy that seemed all out of proportion to the need of the task. She was still tapping the envelopes into order, when she added, "Then I suggest that both of you go to your room, and wait there until I call you."

Together, Slocum and Tollie left the room. A little to the right, through the window, Slocum could glimpse the green trees of the Peppersalt Land, and saw for a moment in her mind, the dark damp shadows, and heard the wind howling like ghosts. To the left, lower down, showed the dry brown road which led to the crossroads and Cicero's store. The air was perfectly still and heavy with midday heat; the shades of green in the trees, in the leaves were motionless and extraordinarily vivid. As the girls left the room under the weight of their grandmother's disapproval, it seemed to Slocum that each leaf, each blade of grass seemed to be living its own full happy, individual life, while she had been exiled into a gloomy world where everything was wrong and at odds with everything else. Near the bottom of the stairs, she saw Megs staring at them from the kitchen, her sharp blue eyes as full of censure as her grandmother's.

In spite of the tension, there was a pleasurable excitement in the air. As they closed the bedroom door behind them, Tollie grasped Slocum's hands, her eyes wide. "Are we going to tell?" she whispered.

Slocum considered the question carefully, as if from all sides. "I'm not," she said, stretching out full length across the bed.

"And I'm not either," said Tollie, stretching out beside her. A moment later, she raised up. "What if they torture us?"

"Oh, don't be silly, Tollie. They won't do anything to us. Besides, we don't know for certain where Howard went to."

"Yes we do," replied Tollie ominously. "We know exactly where he went."

Slocum could not dispute this, and by some strange association of ideas, she saw the human skull again, gleaming beneath its blanket of fallen leaves. In spite of Slocum's deep love for her grandmother and the extreme pleasure her approval gave her, she wasn't certain about her grandmother's feelings and intentions toward Howard Jackson. For instance that morning she'd seen her grandmother look at Howard just the way she looked at Tollie sometimes, looking directly at her, but not seeing her at all, seeing around her, or through her, almost as if she didn't want to see her. Still, part of Slocum was terribly eager to tell her grandmother that they had last seen Howard going in the direction of the Peppersalt Land. But somehow another part of her wouldn't quite permit a confession of this nature. Slocum said nothing, displeased and bewildered by the conflict that was going on inside her. She turned over on her stomach and drew her attention to the world outside the window. She thought again of the meeting between Howard and her grandmother earlier that morning. Slocum had overheard her saying to Howard something about him doing the right thing, no matter what happened. Then she remembered Megs' comment about Howard having a good head on his shoulders. And it seemed to Slocum that both Megs and her grandmother loved Howard with their minds rather than with their hearts.

"Here they come," said Tollie, overlooking the troubled expression on Slocum's face, concentrating instead on the small dust cloud rising up from the road outside the window. "Remember, not a word. Let's take an oath."

In a ritual that was very special to them, they touched their tongues to their wrists, then placed the moist spots close together, one on top of the other. "I promise!" whispered Tollie.

"I promise!"

Just then a black and white police car turned into the driveway bringing a small dust cloud with it. Neither girl stirred. They had been told to wait until they were called.

Then, moving quietly on tiptoe, they went to the window and stared down on Cicero and a tall man in a khaki uniform. At the edge of the porch, Cicero stopped and looked up, and the expression of rage and cruelty which had appeared on his face for a second changed into such a gentle, shamefaced look that Slocum almost felt sorry for him. She noticed a small white bandage on the back of his head. He didn't say a word to his companion but for several seconds continued to stare toward the top of the house, glancing at each window with that same soft, shamefaced expression. Then he disappeared onto the porch, and the girls were left with the muffled echo of their grandmother's voice, greeting the men as if there were someone in the house who was sleeping or sick.

Tollie lay back down on the bed, and Slocum lay down beside her. They gazed at the ceiling for a long while in silence. This waiting was evidently very painful for them. All the doors downstairs had been closed, so there was not a chance of hearing what was being said.

"Why don't you say that you think we're doing wrong?" Tollie asked. "You were thinking it just now, weren't you?"

"Yes," Slocum answered, though she had been thinking about something else; yet it seemed to her that they weren't really helping Howard at all. She tried to imagine what she would have done in the same situation, tried to imagine herself in Howard's shoes, alone in the Peppersalt Land. "No," she sighed, finally, taking special pleasure in this confession. "We mustn't tell, not for awhile anyway," she added.

And after this, Tollie began to expound her plans for evading the questions downstairs, and perhaps even throwing them off the track.

"We'll say that the last time we saw Howard he was heading toward the crossroads like he was going into Budding Grove," she said. "Do you think they'd believe that?"

"They might," said Slocum, nodding, and at the same time thinking how nice it would be if they didn't have to think up a lie.

"No," Tollie said after thinking about it, "'cause then they'd ask how the truck got halfway down the road. Oh, they're going to make us tell, I bet."

Slocum didn't object to this, because she almost agreed with her. They were silent for awhile.

Finally, "You like Howard, don't you?" Tollie asked in a small hopeful voice.

Slocum looked at her blankly for a moment, then nodded with conviction. "Yes."

Her switching the topic from how they were going to avoid answering questions to praise of Howard made Slocum feel a little relaxed, and they talked in this manner, recalling the poem Howard had said for them, and the song he had sung until their soft chatter was interrupted by Megs' voice calling to them sharply from the bottom of the steps.

"Maybe we could slip out the back door and run away," Tollie whispered.

"No," Slocum answered, "but I wish we could get back in bed and start the day all over again."

Each girl gave the other a little push toward the door. Finally Tollie shook her head. "I guess there's been enough running away, and we can't play like it's morning again because it isn't." They both smoothed back their hair and tucked their shirts into the top of their shorts. Slocum said, "Just remember, we're not doing anything wrong. Least not as wrong as what Cicero did," she added, and it was as if she said the last words to herself.

"Then why are your hands shaking?" Tollie asked in a voice which made Slocum feel that she could see the skull again, and the dim green frightening interior of the Peppersalt Land.

SIX

THE TWO MEN STOOD up as the girls entered the room. Slocum led the way, frightened, determined, sorrowful. Public opinion was against her as she could see by the stern looks which Cicero, her grandmother, and the sheriff cast upon her.

"I believe you girls know Sheriff Paul," said Grandmother English, motioning toward a tall, sun-dried man with restless eyes and a habit of looking around the room. He was dressed in khaki-colored clothes with a large black holster and gun at his waist. He didn't seem to be a bit glad to see Slocum and Tollie, or at least he didn't show he was. He just bobbed his head in their direction, then sent his eyes up the far wall past the fireplace hidden behind an embroidered screen.

Tollie and Slocum sat on the sofa in what might have been true sullenness if their grandmother's smile had been less kind. Her eyes were large, tired, and squinted a bit which made her expression even more mournful and in a way, attractive. As she sat in the armchair, she didn't so much hunch her back as slump with her whole body, and all her movements were drooping as if she were very tired. She spoke slowly, almost languidly, but her voice and speech, with its soft, indistinct R sounds was very pleasing.

"These gentlemen and I have been talking," she began, "and we are all in complete accord on one point, and that is that we regret very much what happened this morning."

Slocum looked over at Cicero to see if she could find regret on his face. The white bandage on the back of his semibald head seemed to be occupying his attention. He patted it continuously. Slocum wondered if it hurt. He must have cut his head when he fell backwards into the canned peaches. She felt too depressed to look further for any expression on his face, and tried to turn her attention back to what her grandmother was saying.

" . . . and if you know where Howard is, these men would appreciate it if you would tell them. They mean to do him no harm, but he must pay for certain damages."

Slocum felt a slight stirring beside her. Tollie moved closer and nudged the side of her leg, and looking up, Slocum saw Sheriff Paul and Cicero watching every move they made.

"We don't know," she told them softly, politely. "Howard let us out close to his father's house. He didn't say where he was going."

"It's for his own good, young lady," Cicero said. He got up and stood directly in front of the girls. "As a matter of fact, the longer he stays out, the harder it's gonna go on him."

Sheriff Paul confirmed this with a brief bob of his head, and told the girls they had nothing to be afraid of. Then he asked them to tell the story all over again, from the beginning to the end, and he took out of his shirt pocket a small notebook and a stub of a pencil.

Slocum drew a deep breath and related the story a second time, trying to remember in all honesty exactly what had happened, going on in great detail about how Cicero had grabbed the broom and swung it at Howard.

Cicero laughed lightly, in spite of the flush on his face. "Not a very lethal weapon, I'd say, a broomstick." He sat in a near chair and wiped his forehead with a wadded handkerchief. "Now, young ladies, do you really think I intended to harm the boy?"

"You weren't going to sweep the floor," muttered Tollie.

"That's enough," said Grandmother English, not unkindly, but firmly.

Cicero rushed on, sensing an ally. "Naturally I was angry. I was being told what I could and couldn't do by that young buck. And in my own store! I got rights same as him. He was threatening me."

"What about Howard? You threatened him,"

said Slocum.

"Oh, young Jackson was full of himself, almost as if he was baiting me for trouble. You know that. You was there. But I didn't want no trouble. Trouble was the last thing I wanted from his kind."

Slocum sat for a moment, tongue-tied with resentment. When she was finally able to speak, her voice was, even to her own ears, weak and silly. "All he wanted was to buy some—"

"And you think I was wrong?" Cicero asked, spreading his hands wide, palms up. "What would your grandmother have thought of me if I'd sold beer to the fella who was driving her granddaughter around?" He looked over at Slocum's grandmother, his eyes pleading for reassurance that he had done the right thing. Grandmother English said nothing. Suddenly old Cicero's eyebrows climbed high up onto his forehead. "Well, maybe I should have just gone ahead and sold him the wherewithal to get pot drunk, then stood on the porch of my store and watched him gun off down the road like a bat out of hell. I suppose that's what I should have done." He slumped deeper into the chair, patting the bandage on his head, wincing a little, muttering, "A man ain't got a right to use his own good judgment anymore."

Grandmother English sat quietly in her chair studying her hands, which seemed to be trembling slightly. "We're not saying that, Mr. Cicero," she said. "Not saying that at all. And I doubt if anyone is going to get dangerously drunk on two cans of beer."

"Then what?" Cicero was getting angry. Now he paced back and forth in front of the sofa, still touching the bandage on his head, even patting it now and then as if he were proud of it. "You all are sitting there looking at me as if I done a bad thing, and all I was trying to do was protect *them*." He made a jabbing motion with his finger toward the girls.

"You said awful things to Howard," interrupted Tollie.

"Like what?"

"You said his kind had been getting too much of what they wanted."

Cicero grew expansive. He laughed heartily and turned to Sheriff Paul. "Well, now, that's fact," he said. "That ain't slander, that's fact." He scratched at something inside his shirt and the smile faded. "It seems like if I recall correctly, he had one or two names for me, too." He paused and glanced warily at the girls. "Like—scum."

"He never called you that," said Slocum, incredulously.

"Young lady, I was standing closer to him than you were," growled Cicero. "I guess I heard what he said."

Suddenly the people in the room held no interest for Slocum, nor did her grandmother's look of despair. At times during the conversation when she had seen her grandmother's trembling hands, she had tried to understand why they were trembling, and had tried to understand why her grandmother didn't just tell Cicero that he was wrong. And then she had tried to figure out why her grandmother was keeping so quiet, saying nothing one way or the other. And ultimately Slocum had become so confused in her own mind that she had forgotten everything and felt so sad, miserable and frightened that she simply wanted to tell them that Howard had run away into the Peppersalt Land. However, new thoughts held a fascination for her now. Cicero had lied, and in order to escape from the ugliness of that lie, she was drawn to the image of Howard alone in the hazardous wilderness, combating alone all the terrors of the Peppersalt Land. Now she would never tell them where he was.

"Howard did not call you—that name," Slocum repeated, softly, and she heard Tollie back her up with a whispered, "He did not," and then they were quiet.

Sheriff Paul stood up and flipped the notebook closed. He stuck the pencil behind his ear. His voice was raspy as though he needed to clear his throat.

"And that's all you got to say?" he asked. "Not very much," he muttered, answering his own question. Abruptly he slapped his leg. "Well, I suppose we might as well start looking. These fellas ain't known for turning themselves in."

Suddenly Tollie sat up very straight. "The last time we saw Howard he was heading down the road," she said, paying no attention to the strong looks coming from Slocum.

The two men moved closer with new interest. "Which way, young lady?" asked Sheriff Paul.

"Toward town."

"Are you sure?"

"I was with him. I saw him, didn't I?"

Sheriff Paul looked suspiciously at Tollie. "You weren't quite sure a minute ago where he went. How can you be so certain now?"

"I'm not certain. I'm just telling you what I saw."

Cicero shook his head. "They're just kids," he said, "and I know at least one of them is on his side." He frowned at the girls. "Can't trust young people anymore."

Slocum got the impression that he was pleased that he couldn't trust young people anymore.

"What Tollie said is true, Mr. Cicero," Slocum said. "The last time we saw Howard, he told us to come on home, then he started off down the road." Now she had lied too, which made her no better or worse than Cicero. She stopped short of saying which direction down the road, and hoped, prayed, that they wouldn't ask her. But they did.

"Which way?" inquired Sheriff Paul.

Slocum looked first at her grandmother, then at Tollie. She didn't have to see if the men were looking at her. She could feel their eyes. She lowered her head before everyone else. It was strange that she could see in her mind the image of Cicero swinging the broom handle at Howard, hear all over again the things that they had said to each other, hear even the beautiful but mournful song that Howard had sung for them in the truck. At last she raised her eyes and, feeling sick inside said, "Toward town. Howard was going toward town."

Tollie sat next to her and didn't say a word.

Grandmother English stood up now, as if she were getting ready to dismiss the two men. "That's all they know," she said, quietly. "I think for the sake of everyone we should bring this discussion to a close."

Both men bobbed their heads in a polite gesture. It occurred to Slocum that by the time they got through searching in town, it would be dark and Howard would be alone in the Peppersalt Land, unable to see the snakes, the treacherous quicksand. She suddenly realized that he had no food, no water, and these thoughts caused her to feel an even greater terror.

As the three adults moved toward the front door-Grandmother English stopped beside the sofa and looked down at the girls thoughtfully, and her voice was kinder than it had been when she had been speaking to the men. "The girls feel badly about what happened," she said. "I feel that I am to blame for suggesting the fishing trip in the first place."

So! It had been *her* idea. Slocum's heart warmed to her in a sudden rush of love. She wondered what her mother would say to her if she were here. She had the feeling that she was glad her father wasn't here. Whatever she and Tollie had done, or not done, and whatever was to come, they were in it alone.

"Thanks for all your help, young ladies," grinned Sheriff Paul from the doorway.

After the day had settled down more or less into a hot, droning afternoon, Slocum and Tollie went to the grape arbor at the far side of the house, and stretched out in the shade. Neither spoke. It seemed that if they did so, their distress would break all bounds. They watched how the sun made shadows on the broad side of the white house, how bees hummed inside the honeysuckle bushes, and lifted and almost held still close to each trumpet of sweetness. They watched how the sheets on the clothesline near the back of the house flapped and swayed in the breeze, crinkling into shapes and faces of angry old men, and they kept watching until their eyes could find nothing more of interest and turned toward the dark green border of the Peppersalt Land. Slocum began to think that if she looked hard enough, she could see directly through the clumps of trees and underbrush and perhaps find Howard in the wilderness. She even glanced at the spot in the fence where she and Tollie had entered the forbidden place the day before. And even while she was still looking, her thoughts were very far away from her grandmother, from whom perhaps she had parted forever. And each recollection led her deeper and deeper into the jungle where black moss hung down. She remembered the curious dampness inside the green density, how the wind strummed like the sound of human sighing, and how they had found the human skull. She wondered who had lived inside the skull, who had said hello and good-bye from inside the skull, who had laughed at jokes and felt loneliness from inside the skull, who had loved and hated, and lied from inside the skull.

"I'm sorry for them, Tollie," she said softly. "I'm sorry for Grandmother, and for Howard, and I'm sorry for Sheriff Paul. And that nasty Cicero, I'm sorry for him, too. I'm sorry for everyone. Even us."

And again tears welled up in her eyes—but not for long.

SEVEN

SUDDENLY OUT OF the stillness of the afternoon, Tollie and Slocum saw a figure running up the road. They roused themselves out of their brooding and squinted into the distance.

"It's Mary Jackson," said Tollie. "She's running like—"

Slocum started toward the porch. "I'll get Grandmother."

By the time Mary Jackson reached the front steps, she was gasping for breath, and everyone was there to meet her. Grandmother English took her by the arm and led her to a chair, and asked over and over again what had happened. But she couldn't speak. Megs brought a glass of water, but when she offered it to her, Mary Jackson shook her head and bent over in the chair until her forehead was resting in her hands. Finally she spoke with what voice she had left. "It's Old Spent, Mrs. English. He don't talk no more."

Grandmother English hovered close for a moment. "Is he unconscious?" she finally asked.

"He ain't going to get well. He's going to die," Mary Jackson said without emotion.

"We don't know that yet. Megs, call Doctor Kate. I'll get the car."

In a flurry of activity, Megs and Grandmother English disappeared inside the house, leaving Tollie and Slocum alone with the exhausted woman. At first Mary Jackson seemed as indifferent to their presence as if they were invisible. Then slowly she stared up at the girls with puzzled curiosity, as if she were unable to grasp why they were standing there. She looked older in her grief and fright, looked smaller somehow, a bent, dark woman with a thin strip of forehead wrinkling over deep-set, worried eyes. She motioned for the girls to come closer, as if she had a secret for them. The heat of the afternoon, the mild but pungent odor that arose from her, and the suggestion of approaching death made the porch so unbearable that Slocum would have preferred to move away. Somehow, however, she managed, along with Tollie, to walk close to the woman. She picked up the untouched glass of water and offered it again to Mary Jackson. "It might make you feel better," she said softly.

But apparently Mary wasn't interested in the

water, or in feeling better. "What happened at Cicero's?" she asked, her voice and expression intense with worry. "I saw Howard running across the field behind the house. He ain't come back. Then the sheriff come and Cicero, but they didn't say nothing. What happened? Where's Howard?"

Slocum looked down into the glass of water. To withhold information from Sheriff Paul and Mr. Cicero, and even her grandmother was one thing. But to keep such a secret from Mary Jackson, who seemed to need Howard so much now, was quite another. She tried to catch Tollie's eyes to see what she would do. But Tollie would not look at her, and Mary Jackson's expression held only a merciless pleading.

"There was a fight," Slocum said, not wanting to relate the events of the day for a third time. "Howard will come home, I'm sure. I'm sorry about Old Spent. . . . "

"Spent's beyond help," Mary Jackson said sharply, without looking at Slocum. "But Howard—"

Then there was Grandmother English guiding the highly polished car around to the front porch. Megs was in the front seat beside her. Even before the car slowed to a halt, Mary Jackson started down the steps toward the door where Megs was just getting out to let her in. Grandmother English rolled down her window and called out a series of instructions.

"Slocum, you and Tollie finish cleaning in the kitchen for Megs. Then take your showers and rest in your room. We're just going down the road. Doctor Kate is meeting us there. You are not to leave the house," she added, the authority of her command growing stronger with every word.

"Take us with you," pleaded Tollie, as she started down the steps toward the rear of the car. "Please, maybe we can help."

"Don't be foolish, Tollie. For goodness sake, didn't you hear what I said? I want both of you to stay here."

"Please, let us go, too," Slocum added, her voice sharp because of the tumult inside her.

"No, I need you both to stay here. Now we'll be back as soon as we can. Mind that you do just what I said."

Then the car was moving, slowly at first, and gathering speed on the flat empty road. The girls stood at the top of the steps and watched until the car disappeared over a rise of land. It wasn't the first time that they had been left behind. Almost every day they were confined for one reason or another to the house and surrounding countryside. But it was the first time in Slocum's memory that they had been left alone without Megs to order and boss them about. With this new freedom came a kind of excitement.

Tollie, her dark head bowed as she waited beside Slocum on the porch, was thoughtfully watching the empty place at the end of the road. Slocum looked at her in silence and wondered at the sad, worried expression which she was noticing more often on her dark smooth face.

"They should be there in a few minutes," Slocum said, seeing in her imagination her grandmother's car as it approached the white frame house covered over with a light film of pink dust. "Do you think Old Spent's going to die?"

"Maybe. I don't know," Tollie replied reluctantly. "Everybody dies sometime."

The subject was unpleasant. Slocum moved away from it.

"But, anyway, what do you think? Should we

have told Mary Jackson about Howard?"

"What?"

"Oh, nothing."

But with that intuitive sense which enables a person to guess another's thoughts, Tollie seemed to understand that Slocum was more concerned, perhaps even more frightened than she cared to admit. She lifted her head and moved closer on the step.

"Do you think Howard is in the Peppersalt Land now?"

"Maybe. I hope he wouldn't be silly enough to go into town like we said."

"Do you think the Grandmother knows that?"

Slocum thought for a moment. "She probably does. I'll bet they all know. Oh, they put on a good show, pretended to be kind and not too mad. But all the same, they know, I'm certain of it."

"We can't let them find him." Tollie edged urgently up the porch, her eyes clouded. "You know what Howard told me white men do to a black man who runs away? They strip all the flesh off his back and cut his tongue out."

Tollie suddenly fell silent; her eyes closed as if in horror of her description of the fate that awaited Howard.

"Wha--at?" Slocum asked, equally horrified.

"Nothing," said Tollie, giving a slight shudder.

"No, you said something about—"

"And you were talking about whether or not we should tell everybody where Howard is hiding." Tollie grew angry within the instant. "Howard told me what they do when they catch a black man. Howard's told me lots of things that would make your ears sit up all right. Slocum!" Tollie stopped suddenly in the middle of her thought. "You're not listening."

"Yes, I am. I'll listen as long as you talk sense."

"Don't you believe Howard?"

"I don't believe they're going to do what you said they were going to do to him."

Tollie hesitated, frowning. She sat quietly on the top step, still staring sorrowfully out into the late afternoon. "Things have been different this summer, haven't they?" she said. "Tell the truth," she added, glancing up with a determined look. "We've had more fights, you and me, I mean, and everybody else for that matter. Why?" asked Tollie again, still looking up with an animation on her face which showed she wanted very much to talk. "I waited all winter for summer and you to come. But now that you're here, it's been nothing but fights, and—"

"No, not all of it," Slocum said, sitting down on the step beside Tollie. "And I don't suppose that anything can ever stay just the way it was. I'm glad I'm twelve this year, and not eleven all over again. But the trouble is . . . " and she paused for a moment as she tried to sort out in her mind exactly what the trouble was. "Well, you believe everything people tell you, without ever stopping to figure out if it's true or not, and you seem more willing to believe the bad than the good."

"That's not true—"

"No, let me finish," Slocum interrupted urgently, as if she were about to voice a thought that was close to her heart but which she had long suppressed. "We don't have long talks anymore like we used to, and I guess before I came, you didn't talk too much to anyone except Howard."

"Well, it's more fun talking to him than it is

talking to the Grandmother and Megs. Howard's like me, and that makes him easy to talk to," replied Tollie, who had a habit of explaining more and more frequently that there were people "like her" in the world.

Slocum remembered what Tollie had answered once after an early summer quarrel. Slocum, in anger, had said that Tollie was dumb. And Tollie had replied sarcastically, "Just white folks are smart. Black folks are born dumb. Didn't you know that?" But Slocum was not satisfied then or now with her reply that there were two kinds of people in the world.

"Why don't we talk anymore like we used to?" Slocum asked.

"We do, sometimes. Besides, you might not be coming back here every summer, you know," replied Tollie, leaning over slightly and staring hard at her toes, as if she didn't want to see Slocum's face. "The Grandmother said she didn't know how long she'd be able to handle us. I heard her telling Megs just that. In just those words. And Megs said it was just a good excuse for your mother to go visiting about. But she said it was all right with her as long as it was all right with the Grandmother, even though she said it was getting more and more awkward with us every summer. So maybe you won't even be coming back here next summer. You'll stay with your mother and father, and I'll stay here."

Slocum listened carefully. Thousands of new, obscure thoughts about the future crowded her mind, and she felt sick over the possibility that she might not be coming back here next summer, and felt ashamed that she had parents and Tollie had none. A blush spread over her face. She couldn't bring herself to look at Tollie.

"So what if that's what Grandmother said," she mumbled. "She didn't say it to me." But she realized that it wouldn't do to talk like this, and in defiance of her logical reasoning, some practical instinct was already telling her that there were certain things they both could do to insure their long summers together.

"Come on, let's go clean up the kitchen for Megs," Slocum proposed in a sudden burst of energy. She pulled Tollie to her feet and led the way down the hall toward the kitchen.

A few moments later, after a brief discussion as to who would wash and who would dry, the girls were working busily at the sink, washing and stacking the pretty rose china as carefully as if their lives depended on it. As an extra bonus, Tollie took a broom and swept a handful of crumbs and dust into the dustpan, and deposited it in a sheet of newspaper. There was not much talking as they worked. Words came later as Slocum was smoothing out the dish towel across the counter and Tollie was restoring the broom to its home behind the back door.

"Did Howard really tell you those things?" Slocum asked, ". . . about what they'd do to him if they caught him?"

Tollie, still holding the broom, looked up and the worry seemed to leave her eyes as if she suddenly recognized a friend. "And that's not all," she said, eagerly. "He said they used to cut off a black man's hand for no reason."

Slocum glanced at her in consternation. "W-why?" she stammered, trying to imagine, and trying not to imagine such a horrible thing.

Tollie apparently did not notice her discomfort,

but continued to look at her as if just seeing her gave her complete happiness. "You *do* believe him, don't you, Slocum?"

It was then that Slocum clearly realized that if she was to keep Tollie's friendship, she would have to share her enthusiasm for Howard. Not that this was so difficult. She *did* like Howard. What she didn't like was all the trouble and the fighting and the fact that she had had to lie to her grandmother for him.

"Maybe we should take him some food and water?" Slocum now suggested.

Tollie stared at her for a brief time and then smiled at her across the kitchen, her face restored to its old sweetness and trust. The two girls sat at the kitchen table and began to plot how they could make contact with Howard.

"We can't go back into the Peppersalt Land," said Tollie. "Not tonight. We promised the Grandmother."

"Then how are we going to get the food to him?" asked Slocum, thinking, "It was your idea that we help him." But then she remembered that it had been her idea, and rested her head in her hands, agreeing privately with Tollie that a trip back into the terrible Peppersalt Land in the dead of night was not the most agreeable thought in the world.

"Couldn't we just leave it inside the fence?" Tollie proposed. "Then in the morning if it's gone, we'll know that he got it."

It wasn't a bad idea, and certainly it was a better one than the thought of going back into the creepers and moss, and the tangle of roots and snakes with no sun to guide their steps.

"All right," Slocum agreed, and the girls flew

into preparations.

There was a pleasurable excitement in the air as they made sandwiches, taking care not to diminish the roast to the extent that Megs would notice. Between them a sort of invisible barrier had been destroyed; they now had their own secret, and Howard was a shared property. Two oranges went into the bag, and a handful of Megs' peanut butter cookies, and Slocum took the picnic thermos from the cupboard and washed the inside and filled it with sweet cold milk. They worked together in silence, taking care to clean up the last crumb.

When everything had been done, they stood at the back door, looking out across the early dusk in the direction of the Peppersalt Land. Tollie clutched the thermos and Slocum held the bag of food. A sort of dusty haze filled the air along the far horizon. The end of day. The sky above was grayish-violet; it would be night soon.

"Maybe we should get a flashlight," Slocum whispered, as if the house were filled with people, all listening.

"No, someone might see it." Tollie was quite calm. "We're not going far, and we know the way." She readjusted the thermos in her arms.

They stood in silence before the door, then with an effort went down the steps and out into the evening. They moved quickly across the smooth back lawn, feeling the ground grow rough beneath their feet as they drew close to the fence. Here and there through the trees they could see the small lights of fireflies. Tollie led the way. Thoughts flashed through Slocum's mind, but she didn't dare give voice to them, and continued to follow after the small determined figure of her friend. Close to the woods the sudden screech of an owl caused her heart to skip a beat. When they reached the fence, they found the woods black beyond all expectation.

"Let's leave it here," suggested Slocum.

"No, we've got to go farther. He wouldn't come this near to the house."

"Where then?"

Tollie looked around with the air of an expert, and pointed toward a large oak several feet beyond the fence. "Over there, and hurry before the Grandmother comes back."

The suggestion of Grandmother English reminded Slocum of the house with its cheery light and safe walls, and with the idea in mind of leaving the food and returning to that safety, she grabbed the thermos from Tollie, slipped under the barbed wire, and ran toward the large tree.

Tollie followed right behind her. They listened closely to the sounds coming from deep inside the woods. The night birds expressed their dislike of the trespassers by screeching and trilling noisily. Frogs croaked in chorus somewhere in the distance.

"I guess we should have written a note," whispered Tollie, "so he'd know."

"Well, it's too late now. Let's just leave it and get out of here."

But Tollie kept stopping, lifting her head as if she expected to hear something. Once she called, "Howard?" very softly.

"Good grief, he's no place near here. He can't hear you," pleaded Slocum. "Come on, now. Just leave it, and let's go."

They selected a level spot at the foot of the tall

oak, placed the bag of food and thermos side by side, and on their hands and knees pulled a blanket of leaves up around the food. Tollie sat down and scratched the side of her leg.

"Come on," Slocum pleaded again. "You can do that when we get home." She continually looked around her, searching each shadow, each rustle for the threat that she knew it contained. She wondered where Tollie's fear had gone. As always happened, her imagination far outstripped reality. She heard a hound baying in the distance and was certain that it was coming closer and closer. It was joined by a deep second howling, then a third and a fourth.

Slocum stood uneasily in the darkness. Tollie, still sitting at the foot of the tree, touched the thermos as if to keep it safe. She looked up at the sound of the baying. "The dogs," she gasped. Then she was on her feet, poised in anger. "Sheriff Paul's got the dogs out."

"Come on, Tollie. There's nothing more we can do here." Slocum was begging now, as she had done the day before in the Peppersalt Land.

Tollie spun in all directions, as if she expected each shadow to reveal a snapping, snarling hound. "Why did he have to go and do that?" she cried. "Howard didn't do anything that bad." Numberless and inexpressible frustrations combined to make her rage elemental and awe-inspiring. "I'm not going back now," she vowed. "I'm going to stay here until I find Howard."

Slowly the sound of the dogs deepened until they could hear the shouts of the men commanding them. Slocum looked around for understanding but found only Tollie's silent fury. She changed the subject to the only one that could bring them into some sort of agreement.

"If you'll wait until morning, Tollie, I'll come back with you, and we'll look for him together."

"It might be too late."

"Don't you think Howard can hear the dogs just like we can? Don't you think he has enough sense to get away?"

"Where?"

The question paralyzed Slocum for a moment. She had no idea where. All she knew was that they had promised her grandmother one thing and they were doing another.

Then there was Tollie again. "There isn't anyplace he can go. There isn't anyone but us who can help him."

Slocum moved her tongue but said nothing. She thought of the night and the hazards involved in going deeper into the Peppersalt Land. She thought of the swamps, alive with insects, the fat, slimy green toads. Off in the distance, the hounds seemed to come closer, then recede. In front of them, only three or four yards away, was a rocklike hump where Slocum could not remember that a rock should be. She could hear a tiny chattering noise coming from somewhere—perhaps her own mouth. She felt herself bound together with Tollie, her will fused with that of her friend.

Behind them a sliver of moon had drawn clear of the horizon. Before them, there was that something sitting like a great ape with its head between its knees. The wind whined through the trees of the Peppersalt Land, and there was confusion in the darkness overhead as birds scolded and chattered.

"If only we could warn him," whispered Tollie desperately. "If only we could see him for just a minute."

A thin wail out of the darkness chilled them, and they grabbed for each other. Then the wail rose, remote and unearthly. Suddenly Tollie let out a yelp. Slocum felt the blood rush to her head, and forgetting everything else for the moment, the girls gave a frantic cry and took to their heels.

Safe on the other side of the fence, close to the house, they fell down onto the soft coolness of the back lawn, and buried their faces in it. "What was that?" gasped Tollie.

They looked at each other fearfully, unbelieving. Slocum muttered her reply. "Might have been a ghost." Then she added, as if in shame, "but I guess there's no such thing."

Behind them, on the opposite side of the fence, the howling of the hounds continued. And off in the dim wilderness of the Peppersalt Land, the wild shriek that had so frightened them grew quiet and was still.

They had taken their showers and were just crawling into bed when Grandmother English returned. She came directly to their room and stood for a moment without speaking in the doorway. She was white as a sheet and clearly was having difficulty controlling her face. Her tall slender figure in its mussed, light silk dress, her pale expressive face and her movements, graceful and confident as ever when she straightened the rug with her toe, touched her forehead, took a deep breath, were extremely effective. And yet, Slocum didn't know why, it was just this ability of Grandmother to control herself at all times and in all circumstances that Slocum didn't particularly like now. Megs stood leaning against the wall outside their door and seemed barely able to stand on her feet; her dress was crumpled and covered with something white and dusty looking; her hair was mussed and her eyes were red and swollen.

Spent Jackson was dead. Grandmother English made the announcement simply, her voice as low and drawn as her face. It was obvious that she was deeply moved, but too tired to talk at length. "Get some sleep now, girls," she said, quietly. "It's more important than ever now that we try to find Howard. His mother is quite beside herself."

As she left the room, Tollie rolled to one side of the bed, and buried her face beneath the pillow. As Slocum watched the slowly retreating figure of her grandmother, she felt an irresistible force drawing her imagination toward the lifeless body of Spent Jackson. She did not take her eyes off the door, yet her imagination sketched pictures for her, quick with life and happiness. She forgot for the moment the simple announcement "Spent Jackson is dead," and gazed blankly at images that had nothing to do with death. She imagined Spent Jackson, now in one, now in another situation—bent, smiling, warm, laughing; then she was startled by some feature in the worn face on which her eyes rested in her imagination; she recalled the terrible reality of the day and shuddered, but went on looking. She saw Howard Jackson standing before the counter, saw Cicero looking as if he wanted to kill Howard, she saw the broom rise in the air, saw the uncanny resemblance of Howard Jackson to his father, wondered how they could be so different. Again dreams superseded reality, and it was as if both men were in the bedroom, one on one side, one on the other, Howard glaring in his anger, and Old Spent smiling, and quoting white men's poetry. Finally her imagination grew weary, it ceased to deceive her. She became aware of Tollie's soft sniffling, and became oblivious to everything else. She didn't know how long she remained in that state of dreaming, nor did she know what it consisted of; she only knew that for a time she lost all consciousness of her existence, and experienced a kind of exalted, and sweet delight.

Perhaps Old Spent's soul, flying away to a better world, turned sadly to look back at the world in which he was leaving them.

The floor creaked outside the door, and Megs walked slowly down the hallway after locking up for the night. This noise roused Slocum, and she wondered if Megs would come into their room and tuck them in as she always did. But the footsteps moved on down the hall. Then Slocum was glad that Megs had not stopped off at their room. The first thought which occurred to her was that since she was not weeping and was sitting on the edge of the bed in an attitude utterly devoid of sadness, Megs might have taken her for an unfeeling thing.

Slocum wished that Tollie had not gone to sleep so that they might talk. She knelt beside the bed, crossed herself, bowed her head, and wondered why she could not cry.

EIGHT

THE NEXT MORNING Grandmother English did not come down for breakfast, an event without precedent in Slocum's or Tollie's memory. Megs more than made up for her absence, serving the girls cold cereal and a small lecture at the kitchen table.

"It's nothing to concern yourselves with," she said, swooping the bowls off the table before they had finished, and depositing a plate of partially burned toast before them. "The best sort of sleep God ever invented is the sound and peaceful sleep that always follows strong grief. Your grandmother thought the world of Spent Jackson, so leave her be."

Perspiration glistened on Megs' forehead and there were deep hollows beneath her eyes, and Slocum wondered why *she* had not had a night of sound and peaceful sleep. But she said nothing and ate in silence, anxious along with Tollie to slip out of the house as soon as possible and return to the edge of the Peppersalt Land to see if Howard had found the food they had left for him the night before.

But it soon became obvious that Megs had other plans for them. She delivered the orders for the day in rapid-fire but hushed tones, wiping her forehead frequently with a crumpled white handkerchief that she kept tucked in the band of her apron.

"Tollie, I want you to take some things to Mary Jackson as soon as you've finished eating. Now you are not to stay, but come right back, you hear? There'll be plenty of other people around, but I'm not so sure that any of them will have thought to bring food." A chicken was stewing on the back of the stove, filling the kitchen with a delicious aroma, and through the glass window of the oven, Slocum noticed two pies turning a glorious brown. It occurred to her that Megs must have been up before the sun.

"And you, Slocum," Megs went on, her tongue moving as fast as her hands. "As soon as I get Tollie off, I'll fix a tray for your grandmother. You are to take it up to her, then straighten your room and sweep the front porch. Like as not, there'll be people in and out of here all day."

She bent down suddenly and wiped the handkerchief across her forehead and held it there for a moment. The drawn look that Slocum had noticed earlier was now very much in evidence, for as Megs raised up again, she looked as if she hadn't been to bed at all. Her voice when she spoke was quite changed, no longer charged with issuing commands for the day.

"Mary Jackson asked over and over again last night for Howard," she said quietly. "Now why would a boy stay away when his mother needs him so?"

Tollie and Slocum exchanged the briefest glance.

"Maybe he'll come back today," said Tollie, but she didn't say it with any sort of conviction.

Megs closed her eyes for a second, and shook her head ever so slightly. She was smiling as she made the gesture. Slocum had never seen her look like that before. "Well, I'm not so sure I'd come back if I were Howard. That fool Cicero talked Sheriff Paul into getting the dogs out last night." Megs made a clucking sound and stood very straight beside the table for a long time without speaking. Then she said quite casually, "Well, let's get on with the day. Do not, please, think for a moment," she went on as the girls remained silent, "that I approve of Howard's behavior. I would not for the world approve of willful destruction and violence. But it is a fact that we live in another world, all three of us, and perhaps we could not endure for a single minute in Howard's world." She looked around the kitchen and murmured three words. "Neat, clean, tidy." Slowly she began to smile, a nice smile that for some reason filled Slocum's heart with sadness. "I stand here and look at this quiet room of order, and give thanks that things are as they are, and I hope that everyone in the world will soon know such peace."

It was a prayer of sorts, although her eyes were

open. Slocum wanted to say something, but found it very difficult. Both girls kept still, submitting to a certain kindness that Megs could sometimes display in spite of her bossy ways.

Then breakfast was over, and Megs was all business again, a flurry of bustle and activity as she prepared the basket of food for Mary Jackson, her voice fading in and out as she passed back and forth from the cupboard to the pantry.

"Since you're going down anyway, Tollie, I think it would be nice if you took a bouquet of flowers to Mary. You won't mind doing that, will you? The daisies are in full bloom, but the roses are dead."

Tollie said she wouldn't mind at all, and got up from the table. "Do you want to come with me, Slocum? You can help me find the prettiest ones."

Slocum didn't answer immediately, waiting to see if Megs had any objection. She didn't, except to tell them to hurry along as she would like Mary Jackson to have the food while it was still hot. As they were leaving the kitchen, Megs handed them a clean white damp cloth "for wrapping around the stems of the flowers so they wouldn't die."

Slocum thought, "Dead roses. Don't let the daisies die. Spent Jackson is dead."

They walked down the long hall in silence, and listened to the sounds of the world coming through the front door. Megs' words beat down on Slocum as they crossed into sunlight. But what it was she could not put into words. The dew was still heavy on the trees and bushes; the wet foliage glistened a brilliant green. The sky was milky-blue, sparked with silver.

Very softly they went down the front steps in the direction of the flower bed filled with white petals and yellow centers like small suns. They knelt down at the edge of the bed, picking the flowers a stem at a time.

"Well, what do we do now?" whispered Tollie, pensively, not raising her head from the task at hand.

"What do you mean?"

"You know." Tollie was pleading.

"Well, we can't go now."

"When?"

"Maybe later. If we can get away without anyone seeing us."

Tollie took her time with each blossom, carefully picking only the fresh ones. "Do you promise, Slocum?" she whispered. "You said last night we'd look until we found him."

"I promise," Slocum said in a weak voice, aghast not so much at what she was saying as at what she was going to have to do. Thoughts of the Peppersalt Land, and remembrances of the ghostly cry from the night before were still fresh in her mind.

"All right, then," Tollie said. She turned her head toward Slocum with such a sweet frank look that Slocum for the moment ceased to be afraid.

The front door squeaked, opened, and slammed shut. It was Megs. She called to them from the porch that was dazzling with sunlight; the day promised to be as hot as any on earth. She was looking down into the wicker basket, as if checking the contents.

"I searched high and low for the thermos," she said. "Do either of you girls have the faintest idea where it got to? I was going to send along the chicken broth."

"No," Tollie replied bleakly. "Maybe the Grandmother—"

"Now, what would your grandmother have done with it?" snapped Megs.

Slocum kept still and tried to look disinterested. The thick green grass felt damp through her thin tennis shoes, and a hot wind stung as it swished around her bare ankles. As Tollie and Megs argued on and on about the missing thermos, Slocum studied the objects on the porch; the way the light fell on the aluminum chairs, the weaving in and out of yellow and brown fabric to form the seat and back, her grandmother's splendid potted fern growing luxuriously in spite of the heat, a pink, lace-trimmed pillow for her grandmother's back—all of it somehow strangely flowed together. Why was the expression on Megs' face so stern and cold? Why were her lips so pale and their shape so severe and unbending? And why were there deep hollows beneath her eyes?

"My goodness," smiled Megs, "to look at both of you, a person would think you were mortified to death over the subject of a missing thermos." And that was all she said, but it was enough.

Quickly she dispatched Tollie on her errand, reminding her again not to stay as she would only be in the way. Then she told Slocum to come back into the kitchen and get her grandmother's tray.

From inside the screen door, Slocum watched Tollie go down the road. A mirage took her and plunged her head long into the distance. Slocum noticed how straight she walked, and wondered how she could possibly look up at the sky with all that must be going through her mind.

Megs arranged a simple but attractive tray that reminded Slocum of the summer that she and Tollie had caught the mumps and had spent long days in the upstairs bedroom, being served delightful delicacies on this same wooden tray. Megs talked mostly to herself as she placed a small plate of toast and jam alongside a sparkling glass of orange juice, and a dainty china pot filled with steaming tea.

"I wish I could say that Old Spent died happy," she said, giving a small involuntary shudder. "But I don't suppose when you come right down to it that anyone dies happy. For that matter, there ain't many who know how to live happy."

Megs' grammar, while not perfect, generally did not include ain't. Slocum had heard her use it with the man who came once to fix the refrigerator, and she had used it with Spent Jackson himself. But she was always careful when she knew that Grandmother English was listening. Now she talked as if she didn't care who listened or who did not listen. Accordingly, Slocum sat down quietly at the kitchen table, and watched the preparations. She wished that she were with Tollie and that both of them were lying out under the grape arbor, and that it was the day before yesterday again, and nothing at all had happened.

Megs sighed. "Mary says that all Howard and Old Spent did was argue and fight. She said she never heard such things said by a son to a father." She shook her head. "I'm afraid Howard hasn't made life easier for either one of them. But Howard's like that. He's never been one with the gift of fostering joy and strength in anybody."

Slocum started to object. She remembered Howard's song about "thy soul and my soul" and remembered how his face and the way he had hummed the sad tune had made goose-bumps on her arms. But there was something in the way Megs was talking quietly to herself which suggested to Slocum that perhaps this was not the time for objections of any sort.

Suddenly Megs looked directly down into Slocum's face. "If you know where he is, tell me, Slocum. Mary needs him so. I promise I won't tell Cicero, or Sheriff Paul, or anyone, not even your grandmother."

Slocum felt embarrassed by the sudden urgency in Megs' voice. She noticed that Megs' hair had copper lights in it that sparkled when the morning sun touched her face and head. She seemed so helpless, so filled with a desire to help Mary Jackson that for a moment all the old cold aloofness disappeared.

This simple thought that Megs was, after all, a human being, and not simply someone to be obeyed struck Slocum as comforting; her moist sunken eyes seemed to express a deep but tranquil sorrow, as if she fervently hoped that soon God would once again restore order and peace to her world. All this conspired against Slocum. She was on the verge of telling Megs exactly where she had last seen Howard, and where he probably was at this very minute.

But then she remembered the oath she had taken with Tollie. They had both agreed that Howard's whereabouts had to remain their secret.

"I don't know, Megs," she murmured. "I told Grandmother everything."

"And I don't suppose that you'd know anything about the missing thermos either, now would you?" This was the old Megs, suspicious, bullying, cold.

Slocum shook her head, wondering how large the lie would have to grow before it came to an end.

Things were better in a moment. Megs stared at her, then apparently decided to drop the subject.

"All right, then," she said, "take this up to your grandmother, see how she's feeling, then come right back down stairs."

There were times when it was good to escape, and this was such a time. Slocum lifted the tray, taking care to balance all the objects so that nothing would spill. At the door she stopped.

"Howard didn't mean any harm," she said in a low tone.

Bent over the sink, Megs plunged the cereal bowls into hot soapy water. "Meaning and doing is two different things," she said. Her face was as set and determined as Slocum had ever seen it. "And sometimes helping and hindering is two different things as well."

Slocum didn't say anything. Again she tightened her grip on the tray and told herself it would be best just to leave the kitchen. But she didn't. "Tollie says they'll do terrible things to Howard if they catch him," she said.

"Not true," Megs replied bluntly.

Slocum looked down at the tray. She looked at the kitchen table still covered with crumbs and sugar from breakfast. She looked at everything except Megs who was still bent over the dishes. "Megs, have you ever gone into the Peppersalt Land?"

Megs went on washing dishes. "Now why would you ask that?" she said. "That's off limits—to everyone. Besides I can't imagine why anyone would even want to go into that place."

"Tollie says that nobody can go in there except—her kind."

At last Megs glanced up. Her eyes looked like pieces of broken glass. "Seems like Tollie's been doing a lot of talking lately. I'm telling you that nobody, absolutely nobody goes into the Peppersalt Land, on your grandmother's strictest instructions, and that's that!"

"Why?"

There was a pause, a completely empty silence, as blank as Megs' face. "Because it's not safe," she said, finally. "Now run along before that tea is ice cold and the toast is soggy."

"I don't see why it has to be fenced off all the time. It's not doing anyone any harm, or good," Slocum said, and left the room.

The front hall was still dark because of the many trees surrounding the house. But through the screen door Slocum saw the sun on the road, and wondered how long it would be before Tollie came back. She stopped at the front door, feeling the same loneliness she always felt when she was separated from Tollie even for a short while. Somehow it seemed to her that life should stop, should not proceed in its orderly way, that Megs should not be doing dishes and fixing tea and toast, that no one should sit down or get up until Tollie returned. But nothing had changed in the house, and the thought crossed her mind that even if Tollie never returned they would all sit down to dinner that evening, and beds would be made and floors swept, and nothing would change in their life whether Tollie was here or not; only she wasn't here.

Going up the stairs, it occurred to Slocum that after such a misfortune as Spent Jackson dying, and Howard getting into a fight with Cicero, that everything ought to change, that their ordinary course of life ought to resume its even flow. Bad luck and unhappy days were like failing a test in school, or catching the mumps; once you've done it, then it's time for something better.

After these thoughts which left her more confused than before, she knocked softly on her grandmother's door, looking forward to a quiet chat. When she entered, her grandmother was lying on the bed, fully dressed, apparently dozing; hearing the sound of Slocum's footsteps, she sat up, threw off the light cotton coverlet at her feet, straightened her hair and sat down on the edge of the bed.

As it had happened before when her grandmother took a nap in the afternoon, and Slocum and Tollie had gone to awaken her for dinner, she guessed why Slocum was there and said:

"Well, I suppose you've come to tell the old crow that the day is passing without her. And what's that?" she asked, spying the tray. "Breakfast in bed? I'm not an invalid."

"No," said Slocum, blushing, placing the tray on the small table beside the bed. "I just came—anyway. You're tired, you'd better lie down."

"No, I've had my sleep already," she said. Slocum looked at the circles beneath her eyes, and thought that they resembled Megs' and doubted seriously if her grandmother had slept at all. "Besides, I'm not up to sleeping now," she added, with a deep sigh.

Slocum did not want to leave her grandmother as Megs had instructed her to do, and so she sat beside her on the bed, feeling ill at ease and awkward, missing Tollie more than ever as she realized that in the past the three of them had chatted together, and now there were just two.

Grandmother English took her time over the meal, sipping the tea slowly and breaking the toast into several small bites, none of which she ate.

Slocum felt like talking to her grandmother about the last few days; she knew her sincerity and kindness and hence it would be a comfort to both of them perhaps to discuss everything that had happened.

She settled herself as comfortably as possible on the edge of the bed, and after a brief pause, she asked, "Did you expect all this, all this to happen?"

Grandmother English looked at her with puzzled curiosity, as if she were unable to grasp what Slocum had asked her.

"Did you expect all this to happen, I mean, everything that has happened?" Slocum repeated.

"Oh, my dear," she said, giving her a look of tenderest sympathy. "Not only didn't I expect it, but even now I can't believe it's true. An old woman like me ought to have laid her bones to rest a long time ago, but instead, look what I have lived to see; there was my husband, your grandfather—God rest his soul—a brother, my sister, Lucy, a son killed in the war, your uncle. I have buried them all, and all of them were younger than I, my dear; and now for my sins, no doubt, I have had to outlive Old Spent, too. Slocum, a very wise man once said that there was only one thing worse than dying too young, and that was living too long. But God's will be done. I like to think that He has taken everyone I love because He needs good souls in Heaven, too."

This simple thought struck Slocum as comforting and she moved closer to her grandmother. Slocum watched her as she folded her hands neatly, primly in her lap and looked upward; her tired eyes seemed to express a painful sorrow. She seemed to stare ever so long at the corners of the ceiling as if she were seeing something that was visible to her eyes alone.

"You know something?" she began softly. "It doesn't seem very long ago since I ran races with Spent Jackson, starting at the mailbox down by the road. There was a time when we ran all the way to the Peppersalt Land, then collapsed in front of the fence, completely out of breath, and yet still fighting over who was the winner. Old Spent would stretch out flat on the ground, and look up at the sky and say, 'I won! I won! Ain't nobody faster than me.' And I would answer him in fun and say, 'Most turtles are faster than you, Spent Jackson, most ordinary, everyday, cross-the-road turtles are faster than you.' He would become thoughtful and then, 'Yes,' he'd say, 'but most often than not, it's the turtles that win the races from all the uppity hares in the world, and like as not, it's going to keep on being that way.' And now here he has gone and won the last, most important race; he didn't wait for me. How I loved him! What fun we had when we were your age! But then truly, was there anyone he didn't love? No, I'll never forget Spent Jackson. He was not of this world. When his soul will be in the Kingdom of Heaven, there too, he'll be the same old turtle winning all the important races."

"Why did you say that?" Slocum asked. "*When* it will be in the Kingdom of Heaven? Isn't it there already?"

"No, my dear," said her grandmother, lowering her voice. "I have the feeling his soul is here now." And she kept her eyes trained on the ceiling. She spoke in a near whisper and with so much feeling and conviction that Slocum involuntarily raised her eyes and looked at the ceiling, searching for something.

Grandmother English went on for a long time in this vein, speaking with such simplicity and conviction that she might well have been relating the most ordinary events of yesterday—things she and Slocum both had seen and which no one could ever take it into their heads to doubt. Slocum listened to her with held breath and, though she didn't understand all that was being said, she believed her absolutely.

"You know something, Slocum," her grandmother was saying now. "The big difference between Howard and Old Spent is that Howard suffers from a worse sort of poverty than his parents. He suffers from a poverty of awareness, a poverty of humanity, indeed a poverty of ability to act in a civilized manner toward any human being. Not that this sort of poverty isn't in existence in all people to a certain extent. It is." She smiled softly through her grief. Again she faltered and the smile disappeared. "Old Spent was color-blind. He saw only people, good, bad, and indifferent ones, and tried to love them all the same, and that, my dear, makes him a rare human being."

In a scarcely audible voice she corrected "makes" to "made" thereby confirming again the old man's death. And she lowered her head. Wanting a handkerchief to wipe away the falling tears, she got up, looked straight into Slocum's face and said in a voice weak with emotion:

"I had hoped that I might teach you and Tollie that same art of color blindness, but I've failed, because now I realize that I've failed to teach myself. Being old doesn't always mean that one is wise. Once I thought I knew all the answers. But now?" Her voice fell; she bowed her head. "What is there left for me? What shall I do? Whom shall I love, and how?"

Her confusion was so great, Slocum tried to help. "You said you loved Old Spent," she offered quietly.

"I do. I—did. But I wonder now if it wasn't an insulting kind of love at best. Certainly I didn't mean to . . . I thought all along that . . . maybe what I felt was pity, how terrible, instead of the concern I should have felt. I don't know, I don't know." Her sentences came out in fragments, betraying her confusion. She seemed so grief-stricken, so lost.

"You don't love us, then?" Slocum asked reproachfully, barely able to hold back her own tears.

"The Lord knows how much I love you, both of you, but if I have raised you together only to permit you to be torn apart by the Ciceros and Howard Jacksons of the world, if I lack the courage to . . . " Again words failed her. Slowly, painfully she went on. "If I lack courage in this matter, then I have failed Old Spent, and all those who have died, and worst of all, I have failed myself. But what to do?" Her eyes, gazing down on Slocum, were painfully beseeching. Then apparently she could say no more, and looking away, she covered her face with her handkerchief.

Slocum had no thoughts of any kind; it hurt too much to think about anything. They sat quietly beside each other without saying a word.

Megs came to the door. Seeing the state they were in and probably not wishing to disturb them, she looked at the floor timidly.

"What do you want, Megs?" asked Grandmother English, drying her eyes with the handkerchief.

"Permission to take the car down to Mary Jackson's. I found the thermos."

Slocum looked up. Megs was there to meet her

eyes. She said nothing, but gave Slocum a searching look, then looked at her hands, and for a moment her face and expression had that deep seriousness and sinister cast that always preceded punishment. Slocum dared not guess at Megs' thoughts, and dared not guess where she had found the thermos. She felt that Megs was waiting for a confession of fact.

"Of course, I have no idea how it got out there," she went on, stopping short of saying just where "out there" was. "But I thought I'd take the chicken broth down and bring Tollie back. She should have been here by now."

"I'll go myself," said Grandmother English. "I should have been up and about hours ago." She got up and went to her dressing table with quick steps. The last trace of sorrow left by their conversation vanished when she set about her duties, which she considered highly important. "Why didn't you send the broth with Tollie, as we did yesterday?" she asked, dabbing a powder puff on her nose and beneath her eyes.

"Because I couldn't find the thermos."

Grandmother English frowned at the mirror. "We always keep it in the cupboard next to the picnic hamper. You know that."

"Then how come I found it out by the back fence, gathering dew and smelly with old milk?"

Grandmother English stopped powdering her nose. In the reflection of the mirror, she looked directly at Slocum. For the moment she seemed on the verge of asking a direct question. But instead, she lowered her head and murmured, "The girls were careless again," as if it were a state to be expected and not too much to get excited about.

Slocum breathed deeply, relieved that at least for the moment the subject was over. She was struck by this change in her grandmother, from the deep feeling with which she had been speaking to her, to quarrelsomeness and grumbling with Megs. Watching her grandmother's back as she straightened herself before her mirror, she realized that, regardless of what was happening in her heart, she possessed sufficient presence of mind to go about her business, while force of habit impelled her toward ordinary pursuits. Grief had affected her deeply, but not so deeply that she couldn't attend to other things.

Now she turned away from her mirror and invited Slocum to drive with her down to Mary Jackson's. "It would be thoughtful of you to pay your respects, my dear," she said, and walked out of the door past Megs, who still had the look on her face of unanswered questions and unsolved mysteries.

Slocum paused in silence on the edge of the bed, caught between the stern expression on Megs' face and the diminishing echo of her grandmother's footsteps moving down the hall. Painful memories suddenly awakened inside her. The thought occurred to her: Can it be that one small lie has separated me from Megs and Grandmother only to make me lie more in order to be reunited with them?

Having unintentionally asked herself a question she could not answer, she ran quickly out of the room.

NINE

THEY PARKED THE car a distance from Mary Jackson's house and walked slowly past a solid line of pickup trucks and cars of new and ancient vintage. There were even two wagons drawn by mules waiting patiently in the heat of the day.

"Everyone in Budding Grove must be here," whispered Slocum.

Grandmother English walked beside her, carrying the thermos of chicken broth in one hand, stabbing gently at the earth with her walking stick. She nodded her head.

"This will be a new experience for you, Slocum, but remember, everyone has a right to grieve in their own way, and Spent Jackson was well-loved around here." Her glance seemed to confirm their conversation earlier that morning and the swift inclination of her head seemed to indicate a desire to conceal from Slocum the meaning of her glance.

In Mary Jackson's yard, men stood in silent groups, some in faded work clothes, others in neatly pressed Sunday suits, their heads bowed. There must have been at least forty of them. A few children played in the dirt; a marble glinted now and then, but no one called out and no one laughed. It was as if they had all lost their voices, but not their desire to play.

A few of the men bobbed politely to Slocum's grandmother as they passed, and most seemed to move back as if to make room for them in the crowded yard. Once her grandmother stopped to speak to a small, bent, white-haired man. Slocum was left standing self-consciously to one side, trying not to return the stares of the wide-eyed children, and not wanting to think about what was waiting for them inside the house. She searched the crowd for a glimpse of Tollie, but found no one that resembled her friend. Instead the faces bore that slightly familiar look of strangers that she had seen on the streets in Budding Grove, or in Cicero's store, faces without names or personalities, all the more frightening because of their vague familiarity.

Now Grandmother English was grasping her arm again ever so slightly, steering her toward the front porch and the opened door, and the soft sound of mourning coming from inside the house.

"Give your regards to Mary Jackson," whispered Grandmother English, "—then see if you can find Tollie. I don't plan to stay long." And with these brief instructions, they started up the steps.

A woman sat at the door as if keeping guard. Her head was down, and she was pressing both hands against her temples. As they approached, she lifted her face, and Slocum saw it was wet with tears. "G'morning, Mrs. English," she murmured. "Mary Jackson will be proud to see you."

And with that she ushered them into the dark confines of the room, then resumed her position at the door.

At first Slocum could see nothing except a thousand suns, all resembling the big one that had blinded her out in the yard. Softly coming from a far corner she heard singing. "Lord into Thy bosom" were the only words she could recognize, and then she heard "take him, take him, amen." And this was all there was to the song, but the singers chanted it over and over again in deep, mournful repetition.

There seemed to be people all around her. Arms brushed against her, then moved away. There was a rancid, sour smell in the room, and the smell of bodies and sweat, and something else, strong like alcohol.

Slocum had never attended a funeral before. Now as she felt herself caught in the invisible push and weight of bodies, as her eyes cleared and she saw the outlines of softly moaning women, as the chant of "Lord into Thy bosom" diminished into a low wail, her own eyes filled with tears, and she wondered if she could hold them back.

Through a small door at the rear of the room, she caught a glimpse of the coffin; there were candles burning at each end, their small flames standing erect and unmoving in the closeness of the room. People moved in and out of this room, silent as they went in, some sobbing uncontrollably as they came out, after having looked at what was in the coffin.

Whatever it was, Slocum wanted no part of it. Everything in the room reminded her vividly, unpleasantly of mysteries without solutions and questions without answers, feelings that were new and terrifying to her. She had only one thought in her mind now: to get out of the room as fast as she could.

But then her grandmother was beside her again, her face resolute. "This way, Slocum," she whispered, pushing her gently toward the door near the back of the room. "Mary Jackson is in here."

Slocum started to protest. The dead, hot air caused her face to burn. But then she saw her grandmother's face soften, her firm voice become kind and understanding, and her proud ways all but disappeared as she clutched Slocum's hand with such force that Slocum wondered if *she* were afraid, too. "Only for a moment," whispered Grandmother English. "Dying is a part of living, perhaps the most beautiful part. I want you close beside me."

Together they went into the back room. There were banks of flowers around the walls, country flowers for the most part arranged in glass jars, and empty coffee cans, but here and there Slocum spied a large floral arrangement that bore the unmistakable stamp of a professional florist, with large satin bows, and one that had the words Rest In Peace printed in gold across the front of the bouquet.

Mary Jackson sat erect in a chair at the head of the coffin. When she saw Grandmother English, she got up and grasped her hands and held them for a long time without speaking.

"You come, you come," she murmured at last, her face more tired and strained than Slocum had ever seen it. "And you, Slocum," she went on, hugging Slocum close to her side. "How Old Spent loved you."

With her face pressed close against Mary Jackson's warm side, Slocum closed her eyes and held her breath. Then in a most simple and natural gesture, she put her arms around Mary Jackson and found herself holding on tight. Strangely enough this caused the grieving woman to break into fresh tears, and suddenly there were two women at her side, separating Slocum, guiding Mary back to her chair to continue her vigil.

While her grandmother whispered softly with Mary Jackson, Slocum moved away from the coffin back against a wall and fingered the petal of a gladiolus; it felt like velvet between her fingers. Again she found herself longing for two things—Tollie, and escape from this dreadful place. But still Tollie was no place to be seen, and escape seemed out of the question. She found that her fear diminished if she could but keep her eyes off the coffin that rested quietly a few feet away. As long as no one insisted that she too join the long line of mourners that were filing steadily past, as long as no one insisted that she, too, peek at the person inside the box, she felt that she might survive the ordeal.

Someone had produced a chair for her grandmother, and as Slocum watched her settle primly in front of Mary Jackson, she began to fear that they would be staying longer than a few minutes. She concentrated on the people passing before the coffin.

Some lingered, others hurried by, others dared to reach down a hand and touch. All wept. She listened more carefully than before to the sounds coming from the room, the wailing mournful sound of the women, and even the listening part of her grew afraid. She felt as she stood close to the wall that her body, her bones, her flesh were beginning to part and open up. Spent Jackson was alone in his coffin, and suddenly it occurred to her that it was the aloneness of dying that made it so terrible. No one did it with you, no one held your hand.

She leaned forward a little, one foot advancing before the other. She felt the darkness and the aloneness rushing past her. Her senses played tricks on her, and she began to rush upon the darkness, but the moaning stopped her, and the darkness rushed in upon the sweet sound of music and filled the room with aloneness and with silence.

She searched for a window, and found only blank spaces where shades had been drawn. She raised her head and looked at each face that passed by in the hope that she would see Tollie's familiar one, but found nothing except wrinkled foreheads, and bent shoulders, and tears, and mouths opened in grief.

"Slocum. You, Slocum, come stand here beside me."

It was Mary Jackson, beckoning to her.

She did not resist. The last of rushing darkness fled whistling away. Suddenly a new sensation, extremely strong and pleasant, flooded her heart. The sound of Mary Jackson's voice soothed her, reminded her of the fact that there still was life in the world, and that she was a part of it. Even as she drew near to Mary, she dared to look into the coffin, and saw Spent Jackson as she had never seen him in life. She was filled with wonder as she peered down and saw that he was handsome, almost graceful in death. He was clean, so beautifully clean in a blue soft suit, a smile of peace upon his face which somehow seemed less wrinkled, less worn than before. His head upon the pillow was turned slightly in her direction as if he might have looked at her if he had opened his eyes, and his white hair was brushed and parted, and the candle light shone on his forehead like a star. He looked so young, like Howard almost. It had been the sweat and the endless chores that had made him look old in life. Now he was merely sleeping and so at peace.

Slocum had planned to tell Mary that she was sorry Old Spent had died. But now looking down on his face so strong in death, she wasn't altogether certain that she was sorry at all. If all deaths were this gentle, this kind, if all dead people looked so at peace, so contented, then death must be nothing more than a new adventure of life.

Instead of speaking to Mary at all, she simply went to her side and rested her arm gently on her shoulder. And this simple gesture seemed to suffice, and for a long time, the three of them, Slocum, Grandmother English, and Mary Jackson, sat in silence, and watched the mourners with their tears, and kept quiet with private thoughts.

"I wish Howard was here," Mary Jackson murmured once.

"He'll come back, I'm sure," Grandmother English said.

Mary drew her hands down into her lap. "Not like him," she whispered. "Even though . . . "

"Even though what?"

"I never, I never seen a boy change like that." She bent over, hid her face in her hands. "Is he in bad trouble, Mrs. English?" she whispered, and the words came out muffled.

"No, not bad. No trouble at all, if he comes back."

"Last thing Old Spent said was that he should have beat him more."

Slocum listened, shocked that the gentle man sleeping in the coffin could have said such a thing.

"But he never hurt anybody, really. Couldn't. Didn't even know how," said Mary Jackson, breaking into new tears.

Grandmother English patted her hands, tried to comfort her as best she could. "He'll come back, Mary, I promise, and there'll be no more trouble. Hush, now. No more trouble."

Slocum noticed her grandmother's face contort, as if under a new strain. She held Mary's hands, leaning down to see her face, as if she were trying to feel it with her eyes. She looked as if she were about to cry. "You'd better eat something," she said, kindly. "You need your strength."

"Don't want to eat," said Mary Jackson. "What I got in me don't need to be fed. You know that, Mrs. English. You been through it. What I got in me needs a son close by. That's all. That's all."

Then she bent over until her head was resting in her lap, as if she were trying to hide her tears. "What I got in me lies dead and warm upon me. I said to Howard you don't know what worry is. I said you don't know. You don't know whether we're worrying or not, whether we can or not. You don't know whether we've tried or not to understand, to understand you, and what's changing in the world. You don't know. You don't even want to know. You just feel like you're the only wild seed in the whole blind earth." Mary's voice broke, new tears took the place of old ones. Her shoulders heaved with the weight of her sorrow. Slocum moved back, more frightened than before, and yet strangely fascinated by the spectacle of unadorned grief.

The light in her grandmother's eyes was clouded instantly, whether in concern over Mary Jackson, or fear that Slocum was seeing too much of a kind of emotion that she could not readily digest. At any rate, she waved her hand at Slocum, motioning for her to leave the room. In the meantime, Mary's sobs became quite audible; women rushed in from all sides, confusion mounted, and Slocum felt herself being jostled in the press of bodies, all willing to lend a hand but all uncertain just what they should do.

Then her grandmother was beside her again, guiding her firmly toward the door that led outside, whispering, "Wait outside, Slocum. Find Tollie if you can, and the two of you start on home. I'll stay here as long as I'm needed."

There was a bright look of illumination on Grandmother English's face, and something else, confusion, the old bewilderment that Slocum had last seen on her grandmother's face in her bedroom earlier that morning, and something else, almost anger. And when she demanded in the next breath, "Where in heaven's name is Howard?" Slocum understood the reckless, stern expression in her face, and was certain that her grandmother was blaming her for not telling them where Howard was hiding.

For a moment, Slocum was almost afraid to move,

fearful that another disaster would descend on her. Her grandmother stepped quickly back into the room where Mary's broken sobbings could still be heard above the din and rustle of concerned women; she disappeared into the confusion, and Slocum was alone in the outer room filled only with old, old women holding babies in their arms, and a few men who had heard the new mourning and had come into the house out of curiosity, grief fading from their dark faces as they strained this way and that to see what was going on in the back room.

"She broke," sighed an old woman sitting at the round table, as if she'd seen people "break" before.

"She know that when they git finished, they gonna nail up the lid over Old Spent's head, and then he gone fo' sure."

"It's 'nough to break a soul—"

"And her no-good son done flew the coop—"

"Howard gone, Spent gone, she alone."

The voices rose all around Slocum. She seemed to be standing alone on an island in a sea of ugliness and sweat, and closed shades, and unbearable grief. The heaviness within her grew. She wanted to see her mother, her father, she wanted to be miles away from this place of death and grieving. But more than anything else, she wanted Tollie, wanted them to be alone in some green, quiet, cool place. And with this thought in mind, she ran quickly out of the house, past the little groups of men and children who were pressing close around the front door, kept on running until she was safely around the side of the house away from all the people, away from the candles and weeping, and at last she fell beneath the shade of a large tree and buried her face in her hands, and listened to her heart beating, trying to think only of beautiful things in order to dispel the fear that raged inside her. She felt callous that she could not weep with the rest of them. She felt that something was wrong with her that she could not give in so easily to a public display of grief. But she couldn't and that was that.

A light breeze fluttered the leaves above her head. She rested the side of her face against the stubbly grass, and fell to musing. She tried to imagine the world after a rain. The wet earth, where here and there bright green shoots of grass with yellow stalks were breaking through, the rivulets glittering in the sun and whirling along lumps of earth and chips of wood, the purple twigs of lilacs with their swelling buds nodding just below a window, the brisk twitter of the birds bustling about in the bush, the blackish fence wet with raindrops, and most of all the moist fragrant air and joyous sunshine—everything she imagined spoke to her distinctly and clearly of something new and beautiful. Everything spoke to her of beauty and happiness, saying they were both equally possible and easy to attain. She thought to herself: I must quick go home this minute. But nevertheless she continued to lie beneath the tree for a long time, dreaming, and doing nothing.

She heard cars passing on the road, but did not bother to sit up and take note of them. Voices rose, children called to each other, but nothing was strong enough to tear her away from this new dream of the earth wet after a rain. It wasn't until she heard the crunch of a footstep near by that she lifted her head. It was Tollie coming up stealthily behind her, as if she meant to surprise her.

Slocum sat up, pleased and angry all at the same

time. "Where've you been?" she asked. "I looked everywhere inside the—" She stopped, the memory of her own experience inside the house still fresh in her mind.

Tollie said nothing but sat quietly beside her, her face down. Then, "The Grandmother told me to get you and go on home," she said, as if she felt miserable. There was a pause. "But I'm not going home, so you can do anything you like."

Slocum tried to bend low in an attempt to read the expression on Tollie's face. But she could see nothing except the top of her head and the way her fingers pulled at tufts of grass, pulling, pulling, as if she wanted to uproot the whole world.

"What happened, Tollie? Did someone say something to you?"

"Are you kidding? They don't have to, do they? They all just look at me like I was a criminal, or something worse. Even Mary Jackson . . . " Her voice broke.

Slocum didn't have to ask any more questions. She knew the feeling. It was the same way she had felt when her grandmother had told her to leave Mary's house and go on home.

Tollie went on. "Everyone despises me, and always will."

"That's not true," said Slocum. "I don't."

"That stupid Cicero was there when I left. I wish Howard had hit him harder. And even the Grandmother was talking to him like—"

Then the tears came, more tears, oceans of them. Slocum watched, helpless; she heard the tall grass behind her fill with the humming of invisible locusts. Her dream of a world fresh with rain was shattered.

She suddenly felt very angry. Just when she had made the world beautiful again, someone had to come along and spoil it. And when she saw Tollie's trembling lips and her eyes full of tears, she forgot everything and felt so furious, miserable and frightened that she, too, would have preferred to run away rather than return to her grandmother's house.

She felt contempt for everyone who was grieving in the small white frame house, and for her grandmother in particular. She remembered her grandmother's confusion that morning, heard her say in memory, "I lack the courage . . . " So she did! Slocum began to persuade herself, to the background of Tollie's quiet tears, that her grandmother didn't really want them at all. They were a bother, a nuisance, and she had a strong urge to play some sort of extreme prank that would astonish them all, perhaps shock them, or at least make her grandmother sorry that she lacked the courage.

About a hundred yards below them was the side of Mary Jackson's house, then the front yard, then the road lined with weeds and cars, and behind that a new large dust cloud appeared.

"Look, Tollie," Slocum whispered. "Police cars."

She made a sweeping movement with her hand. Tollie looked down toward the road.

"What do they want?"

Slocum tried to think of an answer but couldn't.

"Why so many of them?"

"I'll bet they're getting ready to search some more," Slocum whispered, "or else they're planning to trap Howard."

Tollie looked horrified at the suggestion.

Four police cars drove slowly past the waiting

trucks, then pulled into the line a distance from the house. Men got out.

"Good Lord," gasped Tollie. "There must be a hundred of them."

"Not that many," said Slocum, "—but enough," she added, ominously.

Tollie sat up straighter than ever now. "I'll bet they think that Howard's going to come back to see Mary," she said, watching the spectacle of men in blue uniforms.

Slocum watched too, amazed at the foolish expenditure of energy. "Howard didn't do anything that bad," she muttered. "Old Cicero baited him into a fight, like he was just waiting for one."

The last vestige of tears still glistened on Tollie's face, but her eyes were bone dry, as dry as her voice. "Howard told me that black men were born for white men to punish. He said a hundred years ago, a black man got his hand cut off for stealing a piece of bread." She went on in a low angry voice, telling Slocum more and more of what Howard had told her, one injustice after another, one cruelty after another, each more terrible than the one before. She looked at Slocum now, her eyes and face intensely serious. "Howard told me not to trust any white person." She paused. "Not even you."

The two girls looked at each other for a long moment. Slocum felt a severe burning behind her eyes. She didn't cry, but a weight heavy as a stone lay on her heart.

"What did you say?" she murmured.

For a long time Tollie didn't answer. Then she smiled apologetically. "I told him you were my best friend, and if I couldn't trust you, then I couldn't even trust myself."

And gazing at Tollie in silence, Slocum returned the smile, warmer than ever. "Am I really your best friend?" she asked, raising her eyebrows significantly and giving special emphasis to the word best.

Tollie nodded, and this seemed to satisfy both of them on all counts. Waiting in the tall grass, they saw the policemen make their way toward the front yard. Men broke away to either side, clearing even a larger path than they had cleared for Slocum and her grandmother. The police swarmed through the yard, a few fanning out to positions close to the back door. Tollie stood up now, one hand against the tree trunk, the other hand shading her eyes against the bright sun overhead. Somberly she watched the scene a distance away. She clenched her fist and beat softly on the bark of the tree. Her lips were tightly compressed and her eyes yearned beneath her dark mussed hair.

"They've come to trap him all right."

Slocum cast an inquiring glance at her as she said this, and felt proud that this was her best friend. Now the thought occurred to her that there must exist some yet unknown reason for the general dislike and even hatred that everybody bore toward Tollie and herself. And at this moment she was firmly convinced that everyone from her grandmother down to Megs, Cicero, even Mary Jackson hated her and took pleasure in her suffering. "I don't belong here anymore than you do, Tollie," she said. "Sometimes I think I'm an orphan, too."

"Maybe you're right," said Tollie, without looking at her.

"Then let's run away, right now."

Tollie didn't say anything; there was a long silence, during which she surveyed Slocum from top to toe with such a look that Slocum didn't know where to turn her eyes or what to do with her hands.

"Are you sure you won't miss the Grandmother, and all the rest of them?"

Slocum couldn't answer this question directly; she did well to shake her head.

The policemen continued to form a circle around Mary Jackson's house. The girls watched in silence, as if brooding about the consequences if Howard Jackson were to return at that moment. One man in a blue uniform started to walk in the direction of the tree where the girls were standing. Quickly they ducked down, taking shelter in the tall grass.

"Lie down flat," whispered Tollie.

The footsteps came closer, stopped, then started off again, diminishing as they moved away from the tree. Tollie raised up. "He's gone, at least for now. We'd better get out of here."

"Maybe we should go back to the house and get some food first," Slocum suggested.

Indignation crossed Tollie's face. "And get caught by Megs? No thank you. We'll find Howard first. He'll know what to do."

"You mean go back into the Peppersalt Land?"

"Where else?"

"But we don't even know where to start looking," protested Slocum.

"Then we'll look everywhere until we find him," said Tollie simply, confidently, as if the Peppersalt Land were a mere boulevard instead of a terrifying and uncharted wilderness filled with hazards and horrors both specific and vague.

They faced each other in the bright day. The sun was high now, in a noon position. Slocum looked away first, pretending to search the distant fringe of the Peppersalt Land. From behind came the shouts of the police. Beside her Tollie stood erect, determined, ready to pounce on any sign of weakness.

"No one can help us, except Howard," she said. "You know that, Slocum. You said so yourself."

Slocum couldn't remember saying this, but if Tollie said so, then it must be true. She wanted to explain that perhaps people weren't as angry with them as they thought.

"We could sneak into the house," she said. "Megs wouldn't have to know."

"Megs knows everything, or else makes it her business to find out," countered Tollie.

Suddenly there was a new commotion down by Mary Jackson's house. The wailing rose louder, as if an entire chorus had joined in. A small parade started down the front steps moving toward the road. They were carrying out the coffin. Behind came a group of weeping women, all clutching at each other, clinging together as if each step was more difficult than the one before. The policemen near the front of the house kept a careful watch on them. Others seemed to turn away in embarrassment. Slocum spotted her grandmother assisting Mary Jackson who barely seemed able to stand at all.

At that moment, Tollie raised her head and looked Slocum full in the face. Their eyes met. "Do you want to go back into *that*? Frankly I'm glad they're down there, and we're up here," she said.

And while Slocum understood what she meant, some overwhelming impulse caused her to turn away.

"Well, are you ready?" asked Tollie.

Slocum nodded, as much for the sake of agreement as anything, and by tacit consent they left the shelter of the tree and started off in the direction of the Peppersalt Land.

Tollie talked continuously as they walked about what they would do after they found Howard, how maybe they could all run away to Atlanta and find a house and all live together. "And then," Tollie went on, "after we've settled and bought groceries and everything, Howard can find a job and we'll keep house for him. Are you coming?" And she held out her hand to Slocum who persisted in lagging behind.

Something seemed to rise higher and higher inside Slocum. She couldn't take her eyes off the little procession that was growing smaller and smaller in the distance. She had completely lost sight of her grandmother. Her eyes filled with tears. "I'm . . . sorry, Tollie," she said, catching up with her.

But Tollie looked at her as if she couldn't at all make out why she had tears in her eyes.

"Everything will be better when we find Howard, you'll see," she said.

They walked silently through the heat of the day, two worlds of private thoughts and fears, unable to communicate.

"I guess anything's better than going back there," Tollie said once.

"Anything," agreed Slocum, with something less than conviction in her voice.

TEN

THEY FOLLOWED the furrows of the fields, watching closely, at Tollie's suggestion, for footprints that might belong to Howard. They tried to determine, as best they could, his approximate path into the Peppersalt Land. But there was nothing to be seen except the hot earth of Spent Jackson's fields which contained new seeds and which Old Spent would never work again.

Slocum continued to lag behind, wanting very much to convince Tollie that she was a part of the adventure, but not knowing exactly how to go about it. Everything that had made complete sense under the tree made no sense at all as they drew nearer and nearer to the edge of the Peppersalt Land. The idea that she too was an orphan was absurd. The idea that her grandmother hated her and wanted to turn her out, this was absurd, too. But just about the time she started to open her mouth and inform Tollie of these new thoughts, she began to realize that Tollie was interested in only one thing: finding Howard and running away with him. It seemed to her that Tollie was aware of these new waves of doubt, and did everything in her power to keep Slocum from expressing them. What tormented her most of all was that Tollie sometimes seemed to be as hesitant and in doubt as herself, but tried to hide these feelings.

"Why don't you keep up?" Tollie called over her shoulder. "I thought we were going together."

"I'm coming. What's your hurry?"

"No need to get mad."

"I'm not mad, just hot." Slocum stopped, and raised her face to the sun; it was high overhead. She swore then that she would never again complain, but what was ahead of them was such a fearsome thing. "Tollie, let's rest a minute. Since we don't know where we're going, what's the hurry?"

"The longer we wait, the harder it'll be to find him," said Tollie. "We haven't walked far enough for you to be tired. We have a long time until dark, and we'd better use it."

Dark! This was a frightening thought, and one that Slocum could not dispute, even in the brightness of midday. She wiped the sweat off her forehead. Her stomach turned over in hunger. It was past lunchtime.

Tollie pointed to a large dust cloud coming from

the road. "They're taking Old Spent to the cemetery," she said. "I'll bet no one misses us for hours."

"What if they do? What if they come looking?"

"They won't. Let's go."

A few minutes later they were standing before the trees and creepers that festooned the green dusk of the Peppersalt Land. There was only the faintest indication of a trail here that dipped below the fence and disappeared on the other side. There were a few cracked twigs and softly crushed grasses, and in a clearing of sand there was something that might have been the impression of a shoe. Tollie lowered her chin and stared at the traces as though she would force them to speak to her. Then doglike she got down on her hands and knees and stole forward a few yards and stopped. "Nothing," she muttered. "He might have come this way, but then again, maybe he didn't."

Slocum stood back a few inches from the partially formed footprint, then stared forward into the semi-darkness of the Peppersalt Land. It looked cool. She tried to summon forth a portion of her old courage. "It kind of looks like a big grape arbor, Tollie," she said. Her blond hair, considerably mussed and damp, now lay limp on her forehead, and her legs were a mass of scratches and old mosquito bites. Loose skin from last week's sunburn was peeling off her nose, revealing a field of dark freckles. She spied a sharp stick about five feet ahead and picked it up without knowing why for sure. She closed her eyes and held the stick close beside her leg, and raised her head and breathed gently, assessing the current of passing wind for information. The woods were very still, and filled with shadows. In some places the trees were so thick that the sun's warmth never touched the earth. In those places it was as black as night.

At length, Slocum let out her breath in a long sigh. "I thought I smelled something," she said. She passed her tongue across dry lips and glanced down at Tollie, still crouched in the sand. Then again she started forward and glanced this way and that over the ground.

The silence of the Peppersalt Land was more oppressive than the heat, and at this hour of the day there wasn't even the whine of insects. Only when Slocum herself roused the sleeping insects with her passage through the brush was the silence broken, and then so faintly that within the moment the sound had died, leaving nothing.

Now Slocum led the way, streaming with sweat, streaked with scratches, her face strained by all the problems and hazards of the day. She tried to keep her eyes open for every piece of damp earth that might be quicksand. The partial trail disappeared a few yards beyond the fence and there was nothing to do but cut directly through the mass of creepers and vines toward the heart of the Peppersalt Land. Here and there the woods opened a little and instead of enormous trunks supporting a dark foliage roof there were light gray trunks and crowns of blue sky. Slocum stopped a moment by a maze of fallen timber and rusted pipes and blackened tin. She didn't seem to notice when Tollie spoke.

"I suppose we should have brought some water."

Slocum looked up, frowning at this new complication. "Uh?" She pretended not to notice Tollie's pinched face and shortness of breath.

"I said we probably should have thought to bring water."

Slocum sent all of her attention toward the tangle of rusted pipes and fallen timber, and tried to act as if water was not uppermost in her mind at all.

"I guess we can get some when we find Howard, can't we?"

"How do I know?" There was a sharp edge in Tollie's voice. She licked her lips continuously as if they were dry beyond description. She looked around with eyes that lacked interest in what they saw, and turned her ear in the direction from which they had just come. "Listen!" she whispered.

Slocum listened and heard nothing. "No one's coming. You said yourself they wouldn't miss us for hours. And even then, how would they know where to start looking? As far as they're concerned, this place doesn't even exist. Now, if we're going, let's go."

This shift of courage, one daring, the other holding back, was typical of them. Grandmother English had said more than once that what one girl lacked, the other one more than made up for, and this made them an altogether "awesome twosome." Slocum closed her eyes for a moment, vividly picturing her grandmother's face, her white hair arranged soft as clouds, with the thin strand of pearls and something pale and pink around her neck and, feeling snug, immersing herself in sweet fancies and memories. Gazing fixedly at a piece of rotting timber, she saw her grandmother as clearly as she had an hour before in Mary Jackson's house; she talked with her in her mind and, although it made no sense whatever, this imaginary conversation give her indescribable pleasure, because the words "my dear" and "dearest" constantly occurred in it.

These reveries were so vivid that Slocum was unable to go on for a moment and longed to share her sudden contentment with someone. But she was afraid that if she mentioned it to Tollie that it would be interpreted as a sign of flagging courage, and from the expression on Tollie's face, Slocum was convinced that at least one of them should display courage. The afternoon appeared before her now as nothing more than a game, an adventure not unlike the adventure of a few days ago when they had ventured into the Peppersalt Land for the very first time. On that day, they had returned safely. True, they had found the human skull, but as Tollie herself had pointed out, there was nothing about a skull that could hurt them. Restored by these thoughts, she glanced up and saw that Tollie was examining the old pieces of tin and timber. Her breathing seemed to be normal again.

"Someone must have lived here once," Tollie said, kicking a small log with her toe.

"No one we know, I guess," joked Slocum.

"Howard told me that lots of people lived here once a long time ago," Tollie replied. "Howard knows all about the Peppersalt Land. He's done research."

Slocum listened intently, wondering where one would go to do research on such a place as this. She remembered her father's version of life in the Peppersalt Land, about how blood ran and children died of starvation. The two girls looked at each other, as if a shameful knowledge were growing inside them, and they did not know how to begin a confession.

"Slaves, you know," Tollie said quietly. "The Grandmother's father—"

"I know," said Slocum hurriedly. "Are you ready now? You said yourself we'd better find Howard before it gets dark."

And without looking back she started forward again, feeling a strong need to put an end to the conversation at hand. She heard a slight stirring behind her which indicated that Tollie was following.

A few moments later, Tollie said, "You know what? I'll bet Megs has lunch on the table. What do you suppose she'll do when—"

"She won't do anything. She'll just think we're with Grandmother, that's all. And Grandmother will think we're home with Megs." Slocum felt too depressed for further discussion of anything. When Tollie asked her why she was so quiet, she muttered something about not wanting to waste her breath on silly talk.

Tollie sighed and wiped her forehead with the back of her arm. The noise the two girls made faded behind them, only to be greeted by a deeper silence up ahead. With the martyred expression of a child who has to keep up with a parent, Tollie scurried along behind Slocum, looking back occasionally, jumping to one side when something unseen rustled through the underbrush, but moving steadily forward toward the heart and core of the Peppersalt Land.

They lost all sense of time. After they had scrambled down several ravines and up the opposite sides, Slocum was no longer certain of the direction in which they were traveling. For awhile, she comforted herself with the knowledge that all they had to do was turn and retrace their steps in order to find their way back to safety. Now she was not so certain. The crooks and angles were subtle, and once they had walked for several minutes only to find that they had made a complete circle.

The afternoon sun slanted in from one side of the sky, and Slocum felt, too late, the sting of a fresh sunburn on her bare arms.

Sometime later, Tollie collapsed on a fallen trunk. "Wait," she gasped. "Let's stop a minute."

Silence now. Slocum looked back over her shoulder. A sudden breeze scattered light over the place where Tollie sat. Slocum was uncertain whether to stand up or sit down. The knot in her chest suggested that she, too, needed a rest, but she didn't want to show any signs of weakness. She cleared her throat and continued to stand.

"Now, what's the matter?" she asked, her voice ringing out louder than usual.

Tollie pointed down at the log on which she was sitting. "Nothing's the matter. I'm just tired. Sit a minute."

Eyes shining, mouth opened, face glistening, Tollie savored the moment's pause.

Slocum gave in and joined her on the log. They were friends.

"I'm hungry," said Tollie. "I suppose we could look for berries."

Slocum stared at the ground, shaking her head. "Some are poison, remember?" The mention of hunger reminded her of her own.

"You know what?" Tollie said. "There's not a person in the whole world who knows where we are." Although she was resting, she seemed more breathless than before. She smiled slightly, then shook her head as if totally discouraged, then leaned forward and rested her head in her hands. "How could they know where we are, when we don't even know ourselves."

"That's what I was thinking about," Slocum said, " . . . when I was hanging back all the time." She gazed at Tollie sitting beside her on the log, then looked carefully around at the surroundings. "We didn't come this far the other day. Nobody knows where we are. And what if we don't find Howard?"

The silence was so complete that they could hear the unevenness of their own breathing. The sun slanted in and cast large shadows behind each tree. There was no breeze to speak of, and the air was damp and close. Slocum felt as if she were suffocating; she pushed back the mussed hair that hung limp on her forehead. "Maybe we should have thought about it longer, about running away, I mean."

Tollie said nothing. Then suddenly she grinned:

"Well, this isn't such a bad place. We—Howard, you and me—we can manage. Howard's smart. If there's food and water here, he'll find it."

"There's plenty of rocks and thorns," Slocum grumbled. She leaned over and rubbed her legs where briars had scratched; she wondered bleakly if she'd brushed against poison ivy. Tollie watched her and fell silent. Slocum went on. "But you're right. We might as well make the best of it." She gestured widely. "In a way, it's sort of like a book, like when we play on the porch sometimes. . . . "

"Gulliver's Travels," suggested Tollie.

"No. More like Treasure Island."

"But it's not an island."

"Well, we can pretend."

This new mood of exuberance lasted only a few moments. Slocum gave up first with a discouraged groan. "Oh, Tollie, I'm not any good at pretending there's food and water when there isn't any. I'm hungry and I'm thirsty, and that's that!" She slumped against the log and took her hunger as it came. The sun sank steadily and dusk moved slowly through the

Peppersalt Land. Now there was a small breeze coming from behind her rippling gently the tall grasses beyond their log. "Tollie, what if we don't find Howard?" she asked, softly.

"We will," Tollie said firmly. "But we won't find him sitting here. Let's go!" And in a burst of energy she left the log and started off at top speed.

Slocum scrambled to catch up. She walked swiftly, her feet inside the thin tennis shoes flinching from the rough earth, watching the darkness increase around the trunks of the trees, and the sun strike only the highest limbs overhead. It was her guess that it would be totally dark within a few hours. This thought, along with several others, gave her the energy to catch up with Tollie, and even walk a little ahead, as if she might, at any moment, turn and block her passage.

Tollie wouldn't look at her. Once Slocum walked so closely in front of her that she couldn't help but look up; she tried to force her to look into her eyes. If Tollie would do that, Slocum knew she would see there her same fears and apprehensions, and Tollie would say, "Yes, you're right. This is silly. Howard can look after himself because we're going home." But Tollie wouldn't look at her; she either kept absolutely still, or else chattered about how things would be when they found Howard, how he would take care of them and find food and water and a place to sleep. But then she would get silent again and not look at Slocum, but keep her eyes down and there was always the pretense that she didn't even know that Slocum was becoming more worried with every step.

They scrambled down a rock slope, dropped among tall weeds and made their way under the trees. Once a low-hanging vine with inch-long thorns brushed against Slocum's arm. It frightened her more than it hurt her, although she glanced down a moment later and saw a thin streak of blood caused by the scratch. A few moments later they paused and examined the bushes around them curiously.

Tollie made an exciting discovery. "Berries!" she said, holding up a bough dotted with red.

"How do you know they aren't poison?"

The bushes were dark green and gave off a slight odor, and the many red berries were snuggled up tightly against the stems. Tollie broke one off and split it open with her thumbnail. The insides were as dry as powder.

"Ugh!"

"They'll make you sick," warned Slocum.

"I'll bet someone's eaten them before us. I'll bet they didn't get sick."

The foolishness of this remark was beyond Slocum. She couldn't even think of a reply. But when she saw that Tollie had torn off a handful of the red berries and was about to eat them, she cried, "Tollie, don't. Haven't we been dumb enough for one day?"

That brought a bright flare to Tollie's eyes. "If you think I'm so dumb, why don't you go on back. I don't need you. Howard and I can get along very well by ourselves."

And seeing that Tollie was already angry, Slocum dug her claws in deeper. "And Howard's dumb, too. Real dumb, if he thinks he's going to hide out forever." Her voice softened. "Grandmother told Mary Jackson that he wasn't in bad trouble if he'd just go back."

Tollie hurled the berries to the ground. Then she

really did throw out sparks. "You tell the Grandmother she doesn't know what she's talking about," she cried. "You just tell the Grandmother that I'm sick and tired of her being nice to people to their face, then talking about them behind their backs. Howard said that's what she was doing, but I didn't believe him. Well, I do now, and I think it's high time," she added furiously, "that you stop pretending to like me and go on back with your own kind, because I don't want you around me anymore."

It had never occurred to Slocum that these thoughts were in Tollie's head. Tollie had lived with Grandmother English all her life and that was the way things were and would always be. In fact Slocum thought that Tollie should be heartily ashamed of herself for the remarks she had just made.

"I won't tell Grandmother what you said, Tollie. I should think that you would love her as much as I do," she added, curtly.

Tollie bit her lips and shut her eyes, shaking her head from side to side as though fighting back a scream. "Well, I don't love her," she said, angrier than Slocum had ever seen her. "And I'm sorry, really sorry that you came with me. I should have run away alone. Now, go on back where you came from. You're not like me, and I'm not like you, and that's all there is to it."

Slocum felt a sudden, uncontrollable anger. All she wanted to do was to hurt Tollie as badly as she could. "All right," she cried. "I don't care what you do, or where you go, or if you ever find Howard, or if you don't. And you can go ahead and eat all those berries for all I care, because I just don't care what happens to you one way or the other."

The passionate noise of her voice raised in fury

echoed off the green walls of the Peppersalt Land. She lifted her head. A hundred years seemed to have lapsed between her last outburst and her first glimpse of Tollie's eyes opened wide in disbelief. Slocum could not believe that she had said those words, yet she had the feeling that if she opened her mouth again, she would say something even worse.

Tollie stood a distance away, almost invisible in a large shadow. Her voice came out a mutter. "Then go on back. I can manage without you. You're nothing to me either."

Slocum was miserable by that time, ashamed and sorry. "I can't just leave you here," she muttered, keeping her face down.

"Why not?" replied Tollie, coolly.

"What if you don't find Howard?"

"I will."

"And you'll never come back?"

Tollie lifted her head in the dusk. "Never!"

They looked at each other, baffled by the intensity of their harsh words. Slocum turned, dazed, and started off in the direction from which they had come. After a few steps she stopped. "Why are you acting like this, Tollie?" she demanded, fresh anger brewing in her voice.

"I'm not acting like anything. Howard said we'd have a bad fight someday, and all the truth would come out. Well, now we have."

"You know what I wish?" cried Slocum. "I wish Howard had never come back to Georgia, or I wish he'd go away and stay away, or shut up. You listen to everything he says like he was God, or something."

"Howard said there's no God, least not for folks like—"

Slocum whirled around, rage in her voice. "Oh,

for heaven's sake, Tollie," she cried as if she'd just heard the most ridiculous thing in the world. "I think you've just plain lost your head, that's all."

A flurry of wind made the trees talk, and the noise seemed very loud now that their voices had ceased. Two branches rubbed each other with an ominous squeaking that neither took any notice of.

Slocum stood several feet away from Tollie, all but lost in the midst of her despair. She thought of leaving Tollie here alone and then she thought of staying with her, and both thoughts led nowhere except to deeper anguish.

"Talk, talk, talk," Tollie exclaimed suddenly. "There's been too much talk. Why don't you just go on back to the Grandmother, and I'll go on alone. That's what you want. That's what you've wanted from the beginning."

"That's not true," exclaimed Slocum. She became inarticulate in her effort to express exactly what she did want. Inspiration came to her. "Why don't we start calling for Howard?" she asked. "Maybe he can hear us."

"And let everyone else hear us, too?"

"No one can hear us, Tollie. We must be miles away from everything."

"No thank you. I'll find him my own way, and without bringing old Cicero and the sheriff and all those dogs down on us."

For a long time there was silence and neither girl made a move to speak. Then Tollie said, "Well, are you going?"

Slocum looked over her shoulder at the dense greenness. "I'm not sure I know the way."

This faltering made her feel embarrassed. "You

go on first," she suggested. "You just go on and I'll find my way out after you've gone."

Tollie glanced about her, as if seeing the same impenetrable jungle walls that had caused Slocum to falter. "Which way did we come from?" she asked weakly. "It all looks the same."

The world, that understandable world of roads and paths, had slipped away. Once there had been that fence, and this landmark, and now—nothing.

Finally Tollie spoke, almost as if to herself. "How can we find out where we're going if we don't even know where we've been?"

Slowly they started walking again, both in the same direction, searching for signs of their own passage. Slocum spoke, her voice scarcely recognizable. "I guess they'll send someone for us soon."

"If they know enough to notice we're gone, or care enough."

"That kind of talk won't do us any good."

At that the girls started to walk faster, aware all at once of the declining sun. In this new mood, all their harsh words seemed to diminish, and together they concentrated on finding their way out, or finding Howard. Again they fell into that strange mood of quietness that was so foreign to them. After several minutes of walking, Slocum stopped, despair etched on her face. "Tollie, we're lost! Everything looks the same. We're just going in circles."

Tollie walked on for a few yards, then stopped suddenly and held up her hand. "Listen!"

Slocum's lips formed a word, but no sound came out.

Silence and pause; but in the silence there was a curious noise not too far up ahead. Slocum gave it her whole attention, and there it was again; a faint plop, plop.

"What is it?" Slocum whispered.

"Shhhh!" Tollie motioned again for absolute quiet. The sound rose and fell, and died again as the wind blew. Cautiously Tollie started forward, moving through the foliage. She took a step, then stopped, then moved forward again. Once she disappeared completely behind the trunk of a large tree.

"Tollie?"

"I'm here." Then suddenly she was yelling, "Slocum, look!"

This time the silence was shattered completely as Slocum ran through the thick brush. The noise grew louder as she drew even with Tollie, and looked down in the direction that Tollie was looking.

"Good heavens," she gasped.

She rushed past Tollie, only just avoiding pushing her with her shoulder. And together they ran, half-falling, half-stumbling, toward the bottom of the ravine.

ELEVEN

Slocum stretched out flat on her stomach beside the stream, completely immersing her head in the wet coolness, vaguely aware that she had seen some movie star do the same thing in a movie about a desert. Beside her, Tollie laughed and splashed, turning this way and that, apparently undecided which should go in first, her feet or her head.

Leaves like faded brown hair ribbons floated on the green low water. The end of a small log rearing up seemed the peering head of a river monster. But the stream was real, narrow enough to jump across, shallow enough to wade in, and totally beautiful as it flowed off into the green-black wilderness of the Peppersalt Land. And, as if one miracle wasn't enough, they had spied on their rapid descent down the side of the ravine, a summer tree laden with sand pears, and close beside it a purple beauty dripping with ripe plums. Even the air here smelled like Megs' kitchen during jelly season.

At length Slocum raised up out of the water, drenched, and let out her breath in a long sigh and opened her eyes. She sat up, streaming with water, pleased with the soothing effect the coolness had on her throat and mouth. She grinned at Tollie, almost laughed.

"You look silly."

Tollie's hair stood straight, up glistening with drops of water. She shifted her attention from the stream to Slocum, and returned the grin. "You don't look like much yourself," she said. "Come on, let's eat."

Then they were on their feet again, scrambling back up the side of the ravine toward the fruit trees. They gathered armloads of pears and plums, stuffing their mouths as they gathered, laughing and giggling as if they were on a picnic in Grandmother English's backyard. Perched on the side of the ravine they ate their fill, mindless of the purple juice that dripped down their chins, staining their shirts, mindless of everything except that the gnawing sensations in their stomachs were slowly being satisfied.

"I told you we'd find food and water," Tollie said, proudly. She discarded a pit over her shoulder. "I told you, didn't I?"

Slocum looked at Tollie, thinking how pretty she looked, her dark eyes cool and smiling under her smooth forehead. It occurred to her that this was almost like old times, like the best part of every summer that they had spent together, teasing each other in fun, laughing, unaware of everything except their own private world. Slocum raised her head. They were certainly in a private world now. The trees were soft and drooping, all bending slightly downward toward the stream. They were olive green at dusk, smooth, and they steamed a little from the recent heat of the sun. She lifted her head and stared at the inscrutable mass of creepers that faced the stream. Banks of moss grew in profusion close to the water, and everything looked soft, and comforting and inviting.

Tollie commenced picking new fruit, searching through the branches and leaves for the best ones. Slocum watched her, thinking it was not going to be an easy night, but she felt a bit of excitement growing inside her as she thought of some possibilities for making it more comfortable. It was while she was imagining two pallets made of fern and fallen branches that Tollie gasped, "Look!"

At the top of the ravine stood a figure. Slocum's breath caught in her throat. Slowly she got to her feet and moved up close beside Tollie. She blinked her eyes and the shadows seemed to shift in the half-light of dusk. As her vision cleared, she saw what it was. Suddenly she giggled. "It's a tree trunk, Tollie."

Tollie stiffened and moved suspiciously up the side of the ravine, squinting into the darkness. She surveyed the offending tree with distaste, seeing for herself now that it was a dead trunk with two gnarled branches extended like arms. She grinned in relief.

"Looked just like old Cicero," she said. "Looked exactly like that old fool Cicero." Suddenly she picked up an over-ripe plum from the ground and hurled it toward the offensive shadow. "Good evening, Mr. Cicero," she called airily. "Want some fruit?"

Laughing, Slocum joined in the fun, and for a few minutes, they pelted the dead tree trunk with everything at their disposal, rocks, fruit pits, overripe fruit, hurling and shrieking with each hit, the purple juice dripping down their hands and arms. They laughed and tumbled and shouted on the side of the ravine.

Tollie spread her arms wide. "It's all ours!" she exclaimed.

"Come on," said Slocum. "Let's make some beds down there by the water."

They scrambled down the slope, dropped down beside the stream and began pulling armloads of large fern. Once or twice Tollie glanced up at the tree trunk that resembled a man. "Do you suppose they miss us yet?" she asked.

"Who knows!" Slocum said, not wanting to talk or even think about what was going on at her grandmother's house. "There, over there is a good place," she said, pointing to a low flat clearing not far from the edge of the water.

They worked in silence for several minutes, arranging, rearranging, fluffing here, and flattening there. Slocum sat back on her heels, surveying their handiwork, which resembled nothing so much as a messy arrangement of fern and fallen branches. "Doesn't look much like a bed," she sighed.

"Sure it does," said Tollie. "Looks just fine."

Now they sat gingerly in the middle of the pallets,

trying to avoid the sharp edges of twigs. For a moment neither spoke, as if they were each afraid of saying the wrong thing.

Finally, "Are you sorry we came?" Tollie asked.

Slocum wiped the sweat off her forehead; even at dark the air was still close and humid. "No," she said, hesitantly. "But we haven't found Howard yet."

"We will. First thing in the morning we'll find him." Tollie was all courage and optimism.

"And then what?"

"Then we'll get out of here, that's what."

"Where?"

"I told you," snapped Tollie, as if she were tired of repeating their plans for the future. "We'll run away, the three of us, and never have to see Budding Grove, Georgia, again for the rest of our lives."

Slocum rested her head on her knees. She heard Tollie's words, but she did not bother to listen to them. Not for a long time, until she had accustomed herself to this new situation; then she sharpened and focused her eyes and ears again. It was almost totally dark now. Once or twice she glanced up at the tree trunk that resembled a man, wondering if she had seen it move. Suddenly up the side of the ravine behind her, she was certain she had heard a voice, not Tollie's, but rather like someone moaning softly. For an instant she was too frightened to move or speak. Slowly she glanced back and saw nothing, but still the sound of moaning could be heard. Overhead the trees made continuous arrangements of shapes and shadows, faces and figures, all changing with the slightest wind, and all threatening. Sometimes they scowled and warned her away from this place, as if they were guarding it. Sometimes she thought she recognized them, as Tollie had recognized Mr. Cicero in the tree trunk, and sometimes they were outlines and faces she had never seen before. Sometimes they weren't even people. They were just shapes without names, like a feeling or a breeze. And she recalled every ominous warning she had ever heard about the Peppersalt Land and she was certain that in all the shapes and figures and faces and voices, there was something out there that meant to do them harm. She shuddered and closed her eyes, and felt a slight ghostly chill run across her arms.

Apparently Tollie was unaware of the hazards of the night. "I wouldn't mind staying here for the rest of my life," she said, leaning back on her elbow. "I think it's beautiful." She was waiting for Slocum to say something. "What do you think?"

"I think we'd get awfully tired of pears and plums."

"Look at the sky." Tollie stretched out flat on her back, awe in her voice.

Where the clouds parted, there were a million stars, blinking and winking; the half-moon drifted like a white canoe cut loose from its moorings. The night sky was a piece of blue-black velvet over which someone had hurled handfuls of fireflies.

Fascinated, Slocum lay back with shining eyes. Eased for a moment out of her many fears, she shared with Tollie the unspeakable glory overhead.

"Wow!"

"See?"

The cause of their pleasure was not wholly obvious. Both girls were dirty and exhausted. Slocum felt the slight stinging of several deep scratches on her legs. The mosquitoes buzzed thickly all around the clearing and left little but deeper silence. Slocum shouted experimentally, and they listened to the muted echoes.

"Do you suppose anyone's ever been here before?" she asked. "I'll bet we're the first."

"People lived here once," said Tollie. "Remember? Like me. Howard said so."

Again came the quiet communion of shining eyes in the dark.

Slocum shook her head. "Just because Howard said so—"

"He knows about such things."

"I guess." In all honesty, Slocum didn't want to pursue the subject. In the back of her mind, the melody that Howard had sung for them was running through her mind, a low minor key. And the words "my soul and thy soul" seemed to be echoing off in the distance, mingling with the invisible moaning. Now she tried to hide the intensity of her emotion by yawning broadly and moving closer until she felt Tollie close beside her.

"Are you still afraid?" Tollie asked.

"No."

"Not a bit?"

"Not much, not now."

A star fell overhead; they watched it until it was out of sight.

"Did you make a wish?" asked Tollie.

"No."

"Why?"

"Falling stars don't work as well as loads of hay."

Tollie glanced over, mildly put out. "Well, we're not likely to see many loads of hay in here," she muttered.

"Besides, there's too much to wish for," Slocum added. "I wouldn't know where to start."

With night came a cool breeze that dried the sweat that had soaked their clothes, and this same slight breeze rearranged the shadows in the clearing so that now and then they had new outlines to contend with. They watched carefully each indistinct shape, snuggling nearer to one another until they were very close. It was a strange, unreal night, with thoughts and feelings as hazardous as the shadows.

"Are you sleepy?" Tollie asked.

"Not really. I was just thinking about Old Spent."

"He's dead," said Tollie, a mild scolding in her voice.

"Do you suppose Howard knows?"

"How could he unless he was dumb enough to go back?"

Slocum tilted her eyes toward the heights of a near tree, searching, it seemed, for a passage through the braided leaves. "Do you suppose he's in heaven?" This thought reminded Slocum of what her grandmother had said about Spent Jackson's soul.

"Who?"

"Old Spent."

Tollie made a funny sound as if she were embarrassed by the question. "They buried him, didn't they? I suppose if you get buried, you don't have any place else to go."

Fleecy clouds formed curious patterns against the night sky; then the light breeze began to drive them closer together so that at times they dimmed the piece of a moon. "Let's talk about something else," said Tollie abruptly. "Do you want another pear?"

"No thank you." Shifting slightly, Slocum drew

away. She tried turning on her stomach, but the makeshift bed was too scratchy and lumpy; there was no place to rest her head. After several moments of fidgeting, she returned to her back and grew quiet. She felt a longing for Tollie to understand her feelings, for an affinity between them such as had existed back in her grandmother's house when they shared the big double bed. There they had discussed without the least hesitation the most intimate and complicated questions, such as what they wanted to be when they grew up, what it felt like to fall in love, what they were most afraid of. Here everything was different. Slocum glanced down toward the stream that sang quietly through the night. She thought about their bedroom, the clean softness of pillows, the coolness of the sheets, her grandmother's face, Megs, as she would come and tell them good night.

"Could you really stay here for the rest of your life, Tollie?" she asked softly.

"Sure I could. Just like those other people did a long time ago," she exclaimed, almost gaily. "I guess things wouldn't be so bad, unless you were here all alone." She looked thoughtful for a moment. "There's one thing we don't have to worry about. Howard said there weren't any ghosts in the Peppersalt Land because all the ghosts were too tired from living to do much haunting when they were dead. Howard said the tiredest thing in the world was a black ghost."

Slocum giggled, thinking about the absurdity of a black ghost. Then the giggle was gone from her throat, emptied out like a glass, smoothly and quickly. "If there were such things as black ghosts, you couldn't even see them," she said, looking more carefully at the shadows.

"Sure you could. You can see black people, can't you?"

Suddenly Slocum got up, annoyed, and walked down to the stream. "Black, white," she called over her shoulder. "That's just about all Howard ever talks about, isn't it?" There was a trace of irritation in her voice. She sat down close to the water, feeling weak. The water was as black as the night and dotted with things that sparkled and glistened. In a way it resembled the sky, only it rushed more, going nowhere.

Undaunted, Tollie followed after her and sat several yards away. "Why does Howard make you so mad?"

"He doesn't make me mad," she said, falteringly. "He just makes me feel—" and she broke off, unable to state exactly what her feelings were. She trailed her fingers through the water, as if trying to stop its onward rush. "It's almost as if he's—glad we're different. All that talk about black and white. Grandmother said that Old Spent was smarter than Howard because he didn't care what color people were. He just cared about them as people, and that made him smarter than Howard, a whole lot smarter." She cupped her hands and took a drink. For awhile she was almost afraid to move, fearful that she had opened up the same old painful discussion that had caused much, if not all, of the recent trouble between them.

Tollie appeared to be deep in thought. At least she wasn't angry. After a moment, Slocum got up and went back to the pallet of fern, stretched out as before, and waited for Tollie to join her. "I guess we should try to sleep, and not talk so much," she said.

Tollie didn't move from the side of the stream. Her back was to Slocum, and she appeared to be bending low over something.

"Tollie? You coming?"

Still no answer.

"Tollie?" she called again, slightly apologetically. "Come on, are you going to sit there all night?"

In the silence, Slocum's thoughts ran around her head. She *had* said the wrong thing. Tollie *was* angry, or hurt, or both. It was hard to tell. She could almost feel the anger coming from the still bent figure by the stream. "Well, suit yourself," she said, finally, turning over on her side, facing the opposite direction. Strange. She experienced a sensation of glorious relief, as if in making Tollie mad, she had delivered herself of an enormous anxiety. Did she really enjoy arguing with Tollie? Did it give *her* pleasure to talk about black and white, to remind Tollie of the difference between them? If this were true, then she was no better than Howard.

A storm of silence arose in the clearing and even the stream and night birds joined in and seemed to subside. For the moment, the girls were a closed circuit of private thoughts with the world outside. Slocum shut her eyes as if she had fallen instantly asleep. But the truth was she had never been more awake, and alert to the smallest most insignificant sound.

Finally she sat up again, and sighed deeply. "Are you coming, or not? Let's look at the sky some more."

Tollie was maintaining a longer, deeper silence than ever before. She appeared in the faint light to be nothing more than a rock, a lump of an outline crouched close to the stream.

Regret now moved in to replace Slocum's recent feelings of relief. "Tollie," she said, ". . . I'm sorry if I said anything—wrong. But Howard talks all the time about—you know what—and you never get mad." Alarmed by what had happened, and the part she herself had played, Slocum became so confused that she couldn't think what to say next. "Well, I said I was sorry, and that's all I'm going to say," she muttered finally, though in spite of the silence she was certain that no one had heard her. "I wish God had made us all the same color," she murmured.

At last Tollie spoke. "He didn't," she said, softly.

Slowly Slocum sat up, deeply moved by the finality in Tollie's voice. At the same time, Tollie stood and started walking toward her. Slocum watched her carefully, this girl she had played with every summer of her life, who'd run races in the dusty road in front of Grandmother English's house, with whom she had whispered secrets beneath the grape arbor on hot summer afternoons and pulled tricks on their common foe, Megs, had found thickets which they had transformed into magic circles, had sampled Grandmother English's makeup, painting their lips pink, had drunk the sweetness from honeysuckle—this girl now stood before Slocum a very contained, calm young woman. She stood so close that Slocum could have reached out and touched her. Yet there was the most terrifying feeling in the night that an unbridgeable distance had come between them. Slocum blurted out the first thought. "You're not mad, are you?"

Tollie went down on her knees. Her voice was smooth. "No, not mad. But do you know what I wished for on that falling star?"

"What?"

"I wished for the same thing that you just wished for."

Slocum looked puzzled, trying to remember her

most recent wish. "You mean about us being the same color?"

There was no answer. Stillness descended on them. Slocum, looking with more understanding at Tollie, saw that she was hurt. She hovered between two courses of apology, or a longer silence. "I don't understand," she began. "Last summer it didn't make any difference, or the summer before that. Just now. This summer. Why?"

Tollie seemed to be considering the question. "Howard told me that white people don't know who we are because they don't want to take the trouble to discover where we've been."

"What's that supposed to mean?"

Tollie shrugged and kept quiet.

"I know where you've been, Tollie," Slocum announced, matter-of-factly. "You've been spending too much time with Howard Jackson." She moved closer to the spot where Tollie knelt. "Close your eyes a minute."

"Why?"

"Just close them."

"Well?"

"What do you see?"

"Nothing, of course, silly."

"All right, now, I'm going to close mine." Released from the problem of seeing, both girls knelt, eyes closed. Suddenly Slocum raised her hand and with the tip of her fingers started tracing over Tollie's features, moving slowly down her nose, across her lips, around the curve of her jaw.

Embarrassed, Tollie scooted backwards, eyes opened. "What are you doing? That's the way blind people act."

"I was looking at you," Slocum said.

Tollie turned away, unimpressed by the silliness. "Do you suppose I could get old Mr. Cicero to close his eyes every time I went into his store," she muttered. "Or for that matter any of the people in Budding Grove?"

"I'm not saying that's what other people do, Tollie. I'm saying that's what I do. And during the winter when I think about you, I think about all the fun we've had and will have again when summer comes, and I think about how I've told you more secrets than I've ever told another living person, and I think that if anyone would ever ask me who my best friend was, I'd know exactly what to tell them."

Tollie smiled. "Honest?"

"Honest."

A tiny giggle arose from Tollie. A few minutes later she had brightened up and was chatting away, describing what she thought was going on back at Grandmother English's house. She mimicked Megs and told Slocum what fun it would be to slip back and peek in through a window and see firsthand how worried everyone was.

Slocum's only answer was a slight smile as she stretched out again and tried to concentrate on the beauty of the night. Suddenly she felt tired, not sleepy tired, but aching tired, as if there was no more energy in her for conversation or settling arguments. All she wanted was to be quiet, to close her eyes as she had done before, and imagine worlds more comfortable, more secure than the immediate one.

But Tollie pursued the subject. "I'll bet the Grandmother is having fits," she said. "I'll bet she's called old Sheriff Paul, and that fool Cicero, and told them that it's all their fault. I can just see them running around like chickens with their heads cut off. I'll bet they're not bawling anyone out with their eyes now, like they did us yesterday," she said, proudly. Then she added, a little resentfully, "Oh, they think they're so smart."

"They're just trying to do their job, I guess," said Slocum. "And they didn't really bawl us out," she added.

"They did with their eyes. At least they did me. They practically stared a hole through me with their eyes."

"Oh, Tollie, you're just imagining—"

"I am not. I guess I know how they looked at me, and they looked at me differently than they looked at you."

"What do you mean, different?"

"Like they were mad."

"Who?"

"Both of them, and even the Grandmother, like they'd like to whip me, or worse."

Slocum exhaled a sudden noisy breath of air. "Has anybody ever whipped you once in your entire life?" she asked flatly.

"No, but they'll whip Howard if they catch him, mark my words." Suddenly she looked anxiously around at the shadows and the night. "Oh, Lord, I hope they haven't found him yet," she said. "Well, he'll just run away again. Howard told me that in prisons, the wardens watch the black prisoners closer than the white ones, because the black ones are so good at running away. So you just mark my words, he'll run away again. Nobody's going to catch him, not Howard."

The loneliness and sense of loss from everything that was familiar to her left Slocum with an aching void. She was in no mood for Tollie's wild claims. She wanted only to put an end to all conversation so that the night would pass and morning would come. "Whether they've caught him or not, and whether he runs away again doesn't matter," she said. "One thing is certain. He's not going to take you and me along with him. So you'd better just get that thought out of your head."

Tollie sat up straight, staring hard.

Slocum returned her stare a little stupidly, but she could see that Tollie was shocked by what she had said. She loved Tollie dearly, and she was sorry that they were arguing continuously, but now she was exhausted and without further resources to deal with the nonsense that seemed to be her only form of conversation.

Just then Tollie was on her feet before Slocum, with both her hands clenched at her side. She moved so close that her shoes were touching Slocum's leg. "Well, I'll just tell you something, Miss Know-it-all," she began. "In the first place, Howard promised that he'd take me with him, and I thought you wanted to go, too, but I was wrong. And in the second place, Howard wants me to go with him, because Howard's like me, and you're not."

There it was again, "Like you, like me!" Slocum's patience came to an end, and a raw, hot temper moved in to take its place. "What would you do?" she cried in an angry voice. "How would you live? Howard's just filled your head with a lot of silly lies, and you've believed every last one of them. Grandmother wouldn't let you go away with Howard, and you know it. Now why don't you go to sleep and in the morning we'll find our way out of this place. And that's my advice to you, and that's all I'm going to say." She shut her eyes for a moment and listened to her heart beating.

Tollie stiffened. "You know something?" she said in a low voice. "You're no better than the rest of them."

"Well, I just told you what I thought, and that's that," said Slocum. She didn't like Tollie's tone of voice, and was irritated by the way she was standing so close.

"You'd better not say anything more bad about Howard," threatened Tollie. "Or you'll be sorry."

"I'm not afraid of you or Howard," said Slocum, responding to the threat.

"You're on their side. You always have been."

"And whose side are you on?"

"My own, because that's the only side I *can* be on. And I'd rather be there than with you with your pasty flour face."

"Tollie, I'm warning you," cried Slocum, exhausted beyond description. "You just get away from me, and keep away, and don't say another word."

Slocum knew what was coming. The minute she was on her feet, she knew deep within her heart that she wanted to fight with Tollie. Then there was one last warning of "Tollie, get away!"

But Tollie was beyond warning. She pushed forward and hit Slocum on both her shoulders. Slocum gasped at the sudden blow, then returned it full force, and the clearing became a complication of cries and crashes and flying limbs. Tollie hit out again, then she and Slocum were rolling over and over, hitting, biting, scratching. Out flew one hand and grabbed Slocum's hair, the other was aimed to strike her in the face. Slocum warded off the blow with one hand while grabbing Tollie's shirt with the other. Only for an instant did she relax her grip and then it was to twist the material more tightly inside her fist. Meanwhile, Tollie, holding her head sideways was battering Slocum on the chest and trying hard to bite the hand that was twisting her shirt tighter around her neck. Slocum felt torn and jolted, found fingers in her mouth and bit them. A fist withdrew and came back a piston, so that the whole night exploded with sudden light. Together they rolled down the slight incline and into the stream and continued the battle there. Slocum felt her face being pushed into the muddy shallow water near the bank. Water choked her; she couldn't breathe, and in a surge of fear, she upended Tollie who was straddling her, and reversed their positions, pounding on her back and holding her face downward in a similar position. She struck more and more, her hands slippery with mud. A knee jerked up between her legs and she fell sideways into the stream, busying herself with her pain, tasting mud in her mouth, blinded by slimy wetness. Then Tollie fell backwards upon the bank; and the anonymous shapes fought their way out of the water, thoroughly coated with mud, unrecognizable, breathing as if each breath were their last.

Slocum was close to tears, but she was still so mad, she forced them back, and tried to summon strength for a counterattack. The two dark figures drew themselves apart on the bank, and stood a distance from one another. "Well?" Slocum gasped.

"I'm ready if you are," Tollie replied, between breaths.

Slocum squared her shoulders, felt a small pain in her back, found her body arched, the muscles of her neck stiff, her mouth gritty and lined with mud. "I didn't want to fight in the first place," she said. "If you'd taken the trouble to listen to what I was saying, you would have at least known that much." Inside her chest was a tight knot that became tighter with each breath. "I like Howard as much as you do, but I don't like what he's doing to you. He's no better than Cicero. He hasn't even tried to understand anybody but himself." She paused a minute and tried to look at Tollie as steadily as possible. "Why do you believe everything he says?"

All the fire that Tollie had withheld during her life was ready now for Slocum. She smiled bitterly through the mud on her face. "You wouldn't understand, would you, Slocum? You have a home and a mother and father, and you know where you've come from and where you belong. You don't see the looks that people give me, because you're too pleased with the nice ones they give you. You have someone to love you and a home that you know is all your own, and you don't have to wake up at night wondering who you are, or where you came from, or how long it's going to be before someone comes and takes you away to a strange place. Well, that's not for me. I'm grateful to the Grandmother for taking me in, but you know as well as I do that's just what she did. Took me in. I'm not hers, and she's not mine; not like Howard is. And you can tell the Grandmother that, and everybody else—if you want to."

She was half-crying, half-shouting at Slocum. Her lip was bleeding in one corner, leaving a stream of red over the mud.

Slocum felt a deep surge of sympathy for her.

"Tollie, I know what you're talking about, I do. But you're not going to solve anything by running away and looking for fights all the time."

"You're saying that Howard's wrong?"

"Yes, but everybody else is a little wrong, too. Me, Grandmother, you. And Howard's wrong because he's not interested in loving anybody, or making peace, not even with himself." She paused, frustration mounting inside her. "He's not always like that. The other day in the truck he wasn't. But—but something's wrong to make us act like this."

Tollie looked at her for a moment, as if considering what she had said. And, finding it as frustrating and puzzling as Slocum, she turned and walked away with considerable dignity. She waded carefully across the stream to the other side. Once on the opposite side, she looked back. "Well, I'll just say this: I don't care whether you like Howard or not, or if nobody in the world likes him or not. He's my friend, and I'm going to stand by him."

Slocum moved down to the edge of the water. "What are you doing over there?"

"I'm going to sleep."

"Are you hurt bad?"

"I'll live."

"Do you want me to come over there, too?"

Tollie raised up from where she had been gathering new ferns. Her face, mud-colored, stared back at Slocum's, mud-colored. "No," she said.

Slocum watched her at work for a few moments, but she couldn't see clearly, blinded as she was by tears. It didn't seem possible that they had ever been friends. She watched as Tollie stretched out gingerly on her new bed, listened sorrowfully as her breathing became easier. As the night grew quiet, Slocum heard in echo all that Tollie had said to her: "You have a home and a mother and a father—you know where you came from and where you are going, you don't have to wake up at night wondering where you belong—"

These thoughts passed through Slocum's mind far into the night. She kept her eyes trained on the silent Tollie and paid little heed to her own discomfort. She wondered why she had not been able to see it all before, and why others were blind to it now.

TWELVE

THE NIGHT DRAGGED on as if to spite Slocum. Once or twice she lost consciousness, but these fitful intervals could hardly be called sleep. Occasionally she thought she heard footsteps in the underbrush, and she had the most persistent feeling that someone was watching them, and these feelings led her to the most terrifying thought of all, that she would never get home safely, that she would die here in the Peppersalt Land with Tollie on one side of the stream, and she on the other, bruised, battered, mud-caked, and alone.

Alternately sitting up, then lying down, Slocum was aware of how filthy she was. She pulled distastefully at her mud-encrusted shirt, once a bright yellow, now soggy and gray from the battle in the stream. She would like to have had a pair of scissors to cut off her hair that clung in stiff strands to the side of her face. She would like to have a bath, a proper scrubbing with hot water and perfumed soap. She tasted the sourness in her mouth caused by the sand pears and plums and decided that a toothbrush would be nice as well. And her hands. In one of the blows she'd aimed at Tollie, she'd taken all the skin off her knuckles; the sore place was red and rough and stinging, and her fingernails were beyond description.

She looked over at Tollie. Apparently she had fallen instantly to sleep; across the stream she lay with her back to Slocum, a small, knotted ball, unmoving, silent.

With the memory of her sometimes clean, neat self as a standard, Slocum looked long and hard at Tollie. Then she remembered with a little fall of the heart that during the last accounting, her friend was no longer her friend; she was certain that it was over between them, that perhaps Tollie would go away from her grandmother's house, and live with Mary Jackson down the road, and never speak to her again, or recognize her at all.

Then she remembered suddenly the street that ran in front of her house in Philadelphia. She sighed and stretched out, and turned her back on the stream and Tollie, trying to fill her head with pleasant thoughts. She imagined that it was winter. She saw her mother working in the broad white kitchen, filling the air with good smells, waiting for her father to come home for dinner. Just behind the house was a sort of shed where the garden tools were kept. You could lie in there, watching the snowflakes whirl past, imagining that it was your own house. You could go indoors when you were cold and look out the window past the shed where the snow was turning the garden into a white fairyland.

When you went to bed, there was a fire in the bedroom where you could warm your nightgown before putting it on. And downstairs in the library there were books, leaning together with always two or three laid flat on top because someone had pulled one out to read and not returned it properly. There were soft chairs and deep rugs and golden drapes at the window, and a fire in the fireplace, and everything was warm, everything was right and good.

Then suddenly in the fog of half-sleep, she imagined that she was in Mary Jackson's house and even Old Spent was there, his worn hands folded on his chest, looking at her from the creaky rocking chair that he had called his throne. She remembered how Mary Jackson had pressed her against her side in her grief, how her grandmother's face had looked when she had seen Spent Jackson in his coffin. She remembered Megs glaring at her over the lost thermos. She remembered many people, but never once Tollie. To the beautiful summers now gone, and to her love for Tollie, she never gave a thought. It was too painful. These memories were buried deep in her heart and she never disturbed them.

Quietly, and without warning she fell asleep, and suffered terrible nightmares. She dreamed that her grandmother was dead on a high bed caked with mud, and into the room two men were dragging a screaming, shrieking Howard, his hands cut off, dripping blood. Outside it was a windy, cloudy night with a howling gale. A dirt path seemed to lead into the room and on either side of the path it was black as pitch, so that Slocum was afraid to move backward or forward, uncertain of her footing. Green moss hung down on all sides of the room, and Megs was standing by the door as if guarding it, an enormous thermos in her hands which she held like a broomstick, ready to swing it at the first trespasser. Above Howard's scream, a low, deep voice was telling Slocum to find Tollie. As she glanced out of the window, she caught sight of Tollie, her face suspended through the branches that were beating against the side of the room. She cried aloud, "Tollie," and in the next minute, she was standing outside a large white house in brilliant sunshine, watching a strange wagon move slowly away down the road. She ran alongside it, trying to peer into the back. There was a coffin with the lid closed. As she called "Tollie" again, the lid raised, and Tollie appeared, weeping dreadfully. Meanwhile the wagon had increased its speed so that now Slocum was forced to run briskly. Just then someone with a white bandage on his head appeared in the wagon and pushed the lid back down, and shoved Slocum away, and the wagon increased its speed until it was out of sight, slipping behind the sun.

Slocum was left behind, but she went on, running along the hot dusty road until she reached a sudden sharp curve. Here she almost stumbled headlong to the ground as she ran, but the wagon was already far away. The dust cloud up ahead grew smaller and smaller, and still she ran, so that when the last echo of the wagon wheels left her ears and the dust from the road cleared completely, she was beyond all the trees, all the recognizable landscapes. She was alone under the hot sun. A wind seized her and tossed her about; it whirled about her legs, hurling stinging sand against them. And still she ran.

"Tollie!" she shouted, running. "Come back!"

She stopped, threw her head back and burst into sobs. She sat down on the ground, sobbing so loudly that the wind grew quiet and listened.

"Go home to your own kind," a voice said in the distance.

Yes, that was what she would do. But, as often happens in a dream, Slocum turned over and roused herself until she was half awake. And the memory of everything that had happened in the nightmare stirred, gave a push, stretched itself and again pushed with something thin and delicate and sharp, and for a moment, lying on the ground, Slocum knew that the dream was not only a dream. Tollie *had* gone away, not far, just across the stream, but that small distance was much greater than it appeared to be. And all at once everything that had frightened her only a few minutes ago in the nightmare, all her fears and worries, even her concern for her own safety became real. She lay there with her eyes closed, knowing where she was, knowing what had happened, aware that she had driven a wedge between herself and the one friend she loved best in the world.

Slocum stretched during the darkness of these thoughts; her muscles, stiff from the restless night, objected with painful cramps, and the sad state of her physical body added to the dark despair of her thoughts.

Everybody lived for himself and his own satisfaction, and all that she had ever heard about goodness and God was a lie. People sometimes wondered why everything was so at odds in this world, why men must suffer and be so wicked and hurt each other; for her part, she thought she could tell them if anyone wanted to ask her. But they wouldn't listen. And suddenly she thought it best not to dwell on such things. If she could only sit up and go to the stream for a drink of water, she thought she would feel better.

Her first sensation when she awoke fully that morning was a dim consciousness that something terrible and wrong had happened to her. Her hair hung in filthy disorder around her face; she pulled at the waistband of her shorts, feeling as if the slight pressure was cutting her in half. She raised her head enough so that she caught a glimpse of her feet, dirty, and bare.

Then a pain, sharp and prolonged, flamed in her stomach and she took no notice of anything else. She was sick, really sick, and the awareness of this condition left her more frightened than before. She lay back, feverish, her eyes fixed in a dull, helpless stare.

THIRTEEN

TOLLIE DID NOT forgive easily. Slocum knew that she would not be quick in forgetting their ugly words and fight the night before when they had tumbled down the ravine and into the stream, intent only on inflicting pain on each other. She tried to turn her head for a glimpse of Tollie, but the smallest movement made the sickness increase, and it was a long time before she could do anything but lie still and wait.

Then the rays of the sun fanned upward from below the horizon. Slocum looked a moment at the growing gold in the sky. She listened carefully for sounds, wishing Tollie would wake up, but not wanting to call to her. The fact that she needed her and that Tollie might not help her was too terrifying to think about.

An endless dawn faded the stars out and at last light, sad and gray, filtered into the clearing. Tollie began to stir. A single bird flapped upwards with a hoarse cry that echoed presently, and something screamed deeper in the Peppersalt Land. Now streaks of clouds near the horizon began to glow rosily, and the feathery tops of the trees were green again.

A moment later, Tollie came sleepily down to the stream. Stepping softly, she bent down at the water's edge and looked across at Slocum. Her black hair was matted around her forehead. Her face looked puffy and the cut on her lip had turned purple. She seemed perfectly composed, but her dark, slightly squinting eyes glittered strangely from beneath their swollen lids.

"I thought you were going on back to the Grandmother's house," she said coldly, bending over the water.

Slocum tried to make her tongue work, but her mouth was hopelessly dry and no words came out. Tollie, after a glance of inquiry at the silent Slocum shrugged her shoulders, and scooped water by the handfuls and splashed it over her face. She seated herself beside the stream and started washing her arms.

"Tollie, I'm sorry about last night," Slocum began. Every breath was an effort, and she stopped trying to talk as she felt tears coming.

"Last night was last night," Tollie said flatly.

"It's over, and that's that." She went on washing the dirt from her arms, not once looking at Slocum.

Slocum said a quiet prayer to herself. She looked at the face across the stream, so different from the face she had known and loved.

"Please come home with me," she murmured, trying to turn on her side.

"No thank you. But if you don't mind, I'll come over to your side long enough to get some pears, then I'll be on my way. Howard can't be far. I'll find him soon."

Slocum started to protest, but found she lacked the energy. The suggestion of pears caused the cramps in her stomach to increase; she felt her cheeks alternately burn, then freeze. All she could do was lie still and watch Tollie going about the preparations for the morning as if they were back in their own bedroom, washing up for Megs' breakfast.

Tollie crossed the stream and circled wide around Slocum, eyeing her quizzically. "You just going to lie there all morning? If I were you, I'd start on back. The Grandmother's probably having a heart attack by now."

Slocum remembered her dream from the night before, saw her grandmother dead on a high bed caked with mud. She cleared her throat and spoke in a queer, tight voice. "I dreamed she was dead."

"Uh?"

"Grandmother—dead. Last night I had a dream, and she was dead."

The vivid horror of this, so frankly announced held Tollie silent for a moment. "I didn't mean really dead," she muttered. "I just meant—" She broke off, as if uncertain of her thoughts. Then she scrambled back up the ravine toward the fruit trees. "Do you want some?" she called out.

Sickness rose in Slocum's throat. The rancid taste of half-ripe fruit filled her mouth. Suddenly she realized that it was the sand pears from the night before that were causing the unbearable stomach cramps. She rolled to one side, unable to speak.

"Suit yourself," Tollie said. "But if I were you, I wouldn't wait around for bacon and eggs."

Tollie filled her pockets with the fruit, then started down the ravine, still chewing. "That must have been some nightmare you had," she said.

Slocum nodded in subdued agreement. She tried to hold as still as possible, hoping the pain would go away, or at least subside. While she didn't want to reopen the unpleasant subject from the night before, she felt she had to say something. She spoke again, hoarsely. "Tollie, you said last night that I didn't understand how it felt not to belong anyplace."

Tollie turned away, silent. Then her voice came again on a peak of feeling. "I said just forget about last night. You hear?"

"How can I?" pleaded Slocum.

"It's easy. Just get up and go on back to the Grandmother, and I'll go on my way and find Howard, and by tonight neither one of us will remember a thing about the other." There was something less than conviction in Tollie's voice as she spoke. Still she started back across the stream, moving steadily away from Slocum as if she really meant what she had said. "I'd imagine," she called back over her shoulder, "that if you'd turn around and go back the way we came that you'll find the road soon enough."

"What are you going to do?" Slocum asked

weakly, new cramps moving in to take the place of those that were subsiding.

"I told you," Tollie said, as if she were running out of patience. "I'm going to find Howard. You deaf this morning?" She started across the stream, her eyes squinted against the swiftly rising sun. But for a moment she seemed unwilling to move. She watched closely the stream and the spot slightly beyond it. "Slocum? Are you all right?"

A nod would have to suffice. Whatever else might happen, Slocum did not want Tollie to know that she was sick. Then, if she stayed, Slocum would never know whether she had done it out of pity, or worse, a sense of duty, or whether she had stayed because she wanted to. As if to prove to Tollie that she was feeling fine, Slocum pulled herself to a sitting position. "I'm fine," she called, as cheerily as the cramps would permit. "I hope you find Howard soon. What do you want me to tell Grandmother to do with your things?"

Tollie stared. "My things?"

"Your clothes, books, all the stuff on your side of the dresser." Slocum watched closely for the smallest sign that Tollie was weakening. At the mention of their room and all their belongings, she thought she saw a shadow cross Tollie's face.

But within the moment it was gone. "Just tell her to put them in boxes and as soon as Howard and I get an address, I'll send for them."

"Tollie?"

"Now what?"

Slocum closed her eyes for a moment, frightened at seeing two Tollies across the stream. She tried to clear her head and think up an excuse for detaining her a while longer. "Do—do you feel all right?"

"Sure. I feel fine. Why?"

"I just wondered. At least I can tell Grandmother that you were all right the last time I saw you. She'll want to know."

A cold suspicious look crossed Tollie's face. She turned abruptly and started off into the wilderness beyond the clearing. "See you," she called back, almost gaily.

Despair moved in to join Slocum's physical discomfort. She watched Tollie bend low and sweep aside a hanging creeper. She started to call out again, but everything she thought of to say sounded stupid and senseless. She closed her eyes and rested her head on her knees, viewing the scene sideways, the tall green trees, dazzling in the fresh morning light, and Tollie slowly slipping from sight behind them, patches of her shirt still visible between the patterns of foliage.

And all at once Slocum felt that something of the utmost importance was taking place in her heart—that her whole future life was being weighed in the balance and that the slightest effort would tip the scale. She made the effort. She decided to talk to God, whose presence she had so intensely denied earlier that morning. She did not know a great deal about praying except the kind that went on in church, and she wasn't certain that she knew the proper words to get God's attention. All she knew was that someone dearer to her than her own life was slipping away through the wilderness of the Peppersalt Land, and she was powerless to stop her and bring her back. On that note of despair, she closed her eyes and began whispering, "Please, I'm here to ask You to forgive me for all the things I've done and said that were wrong. And I came to ask You to take care of Tollie and look after her. And if You can hear me, please tell me what to do, because I don't know anymore."

She stopped her whispering long enough to listen. Then came a longer interval of silence, followed by fresh rustling as Tollie moved farther and farther away. The intervals grew longer and longer, and finally all was quiet.

Slocum struggled to her knees, one hand holding back her hair, the other clenched in her lap. She would not allow herself to cry. This was not the time for tears. She was alone now, and in need, and obviously there was no one to help her, but herself. On this strong note, she tried to stand up, and the cramps followed her, lodging in her legs and the back of her neck. She put out her hand, timidly, toward the water as if to beckon it to come closer. She looked over her shoulder at the fruit trees growing on the side of the incline. Should she eat the fruit or not? Should she drink the water from the stream or not? What exactly was it that had made her so sick? And she was sick and feeling genuine and acute pain, more pain than she'd ever felt in her entire life. Balanced on a high peak of need, agonized by indecision, she went back down on her knees and crawled to the edge of the water and plunged her face into the sweet coolness, thinking, "Why was everything so terrible? Why should all this be?"

She felt a deeper sickness that had nothing to do with the cramps in her stomach. And she could find no answers to her questions.

The water soothed her, cooled her burning throat, and gave her new, if temporary strength. She turned away from the stream, and went where the just perceptible path led her, following Tollie's instructions, moving back in the direction from which they had come. She stopped frequently for breath and to listen to the curious sounds coming from the Peppersalt Land. In order to lighten her spirits, she tried to imagine her homecoming, saw in her mind Megs and her grandmother rushing across the smooth back lawn, kindness and concern in their faces, scooping her up and carrying her gently to the comfort of her bed, serving her wonderful delicacies on the wooden tray, telling her not to think anymore about Tollie and unanswerable questions. These were good dreams that renewed her courage and allowed her to continue walking, one foot in front of the other, even when the cramps in her stomach returned and strange birds screamed down at her.

She walked until the new strength was exhausted. Since she was certain that she had not gone far, and was equally certain that she could go no farther, at least for the moment, she sat down near the far side of an open space; here a patch of rock broke through the surface and would not allow more than a few plants and ferns to grow. The whole clearing was walled with dark aromatic bushes, and was a bowl of heat and light. A great tree, fallen across one corner, leaned against the trees that still stood, and a rapid climber flaunted red blossoms right to the top.

Slocum stopped here. She looked over her shoulder, as Tollie had done so frequently the day before, and glanced swiftly around to confirm that she was utterly alone. For a moment, her thoughts were almost furtive. The creepers and the bushes were so close together that she could scarcely see anything outside of the clearing. New fears moved in to take the place of old ones. She remembered the human skull, the hollow eyes staring up from a bed of fallen leaves, the rustle of snakes. She remembered what Tollie had said about black ghosts, and remembering all this and more, she held still and listened. Holding her breath, she cocked a critical ear at the sounds of the Peppersalt Land.

Midmorning was advancing, the sun rising higher, the sound of the birds, the bee sounds, even the beating of Slocum's heart was growing louder. She moved closer to the protection of the rock as if she wanted to crawl beneath it. The sun in her eyes reminded her how time was passing, that if she gave in to her fears and stayed here huddled close to the rock, there was no hope for her at all. Still she could not move, and in the most terrifying moment of all she saw her own skull, hollow-eyed, staring up from a bed of fallen leaves. She paused, growing even more frightened as she remembered her dream from the night before. At least part of it had come true. Tollie had gone away, not in the back of a wagon or in a coffin, but rather into the hostile and threatening wilderness of the Peppersalt Land. Slocum closed her eyes and gave in to tears, the tears that she had vowed to keep back.

Then it was over, the silliness of tears, and Slocum looked up at the hopelessness of her situation. She was surrounded on all sides by chasms of empty air. There was nowhere to hide, even if she did not have to go on. And since there was no place to hide, and since she *did* have to go on, she struggled to her feet again, peering around the rock, seeing only the pink and gold tumbled rays of the sun. She made a concerted effort to move faster now, gathering the last shreds of her courage about her, determined not to give in again to her imagination.

But with the first step she stopped. There was a distant rustling noise far behind her, the cracking of twigs, the sound of someone or something fighting a way through the denseness of the woods. She stood silent, listening. The noise ceased, and then there were only the sounds that Slocum had grown quite accustomed to. "I imagined it," she said shakily to herself. She surprised herself, not so much by the quality of her voice, which was even, but by her willingness to believe that it was only her imagination.

But after three more steps, she stopped again, paralyzed by fear, hung there immovable by the sound in the distance of someone coming closer. Suddenly she found herself running at top speed among the fallen trees of the Peppersalt Land. She heard another creature crying out and, leaping over each and every obstacle that was in her path, she ran as if for her life from the noise behind her. Frequently she looked over her shoulder, expecting to see at any moment a black ghost, or worse, a monster shrouded in green moss. And it was during one of these moments when her eyes were trained on the world behind her that she tripped suddenly over an exposed root, fell hard face down onto the dirt, and found herself without breath or energy to go any further. The wind had been knocked out of her, and for a few minutes she thought she was suffocating. Beyond the screen of leaves the sunlight pelted down and butterflies danced their endless dance. The sweat ran down her face, and her knees throbbed with fresh cuts. She looked up, feeling the weight of her head and wet hair and gazed at the sky. There would be no more running. Whatever was out there would just have to come. She lowered her head, carefully keeping her eyes shut, then sheltered them with her hands.

At last she gave up and looked back over her shoulder. Quite clearly and emphatically, and only a few yards away from the place where she had fallen, a stick cracked. The blood roared again in Slocum's ears, confused images chased each other through her mind. A wave of heated air trembled above the earth. There were no shadows coming from the place behind her; only a strange light that seemed to come from everywhere at once. Again, a stick cracked. Someone whimpered.

Slocum pulled herself to a sitting position, training her eyes on the black and iridescent green, seeing nothing yet, but ready to see the worst.

Then the woods nearby burst open. A figure stumbled toward her. Slocum stared, her gaze held by an ancient, inescapable recognition. It was Tollie. Her face was contorted with pain, her arms clutching at her stomach. Her head was tilted slightly upward as if she were struggling for breath. Her mouth labored, brought forth audible words.

"My stomach hurts."

Slocum stared, seeing but not believing. Then suddenly she lay back on the ground and laughed. She laughed, then cried, then laughed again so hard that the breath caught in her throat. The green and blue above her melted into a whirling, spinning blur. And for several long moments, the Peppersalt Land echoed with the sound of her laughter.

Tollie's head wobbled as she sank down a few feet away from Slocum. Her eyes were half-closed as though she were imitating Slocum from earlier that morning. "Don't see what's so funny," she muttered.

But Slocum couldn't answer her. All available breath was going to the waves of hysterical laughter that blended dangerously with new tears. Slocum reached out and grasped Tollie's hand, as if to pull her closer to the merriment. She couldn't have told Tollie what was so funny, even if she had had the breath to speak. It just seemed to her that after so much, laughter was the only thing that made any sense. Too many sand pears and ripe plums had reunited them; mutual stomach aches had brought them together again, and that, according to Slocum's way of thinking, was hilarious; funny and sad all at the same time.

"Come over here, Tollie," she whispered, with what was left of her breath. And as Tollie did as she was told, Slocum made an even greater effort to keep back her tears, ashamed of crying at such a time.

They lay close together, heads touching, hands clasped.

It was quite apparent that Tollie was not in the mood for talking, so Slocum kept still and watched their surroundings out of the corners of her eyes. Strange. There were no threats in the shadows now, in the dancing butterflies or the humming of the bees. The whole world became as peaceful and as quiet as the air inside their clearing.

Tollie fell asleep, and although Slocum vowed to keep awake, her own eyes grew heavy, and she felt herself becoming genuinely sleepy, not the restless, angry, fear-ridden sleep of the night before. She had planned only to rest her eyes for a moment by closing them. But then she found herself at the beginning of a cool dark tunnel, and stepped inside and fell asleep.

She dreamed, a strange, unreasonable dream consisting primarily of all the faces that had caused her such grief. In this wildest dream of all, she saw, quite clearly, Cicero, the white bandage still in place on his bald head, scoop Tollie up in his arms, kindness and concern in his eyes. And coming toward Slocum, the same kindness and concern imprinted on his strong dark features, was Howard Jackson.

FOURTEEN

DARKNESS CAME that day quicker than it ever had before. One minute Slocum was lying on her back in the Peppersalt Land, gazing up, blinded by the high sun. And the next minute she was lying on something soft and cool, in a room dim with evening light, a room that smelled and felt remarkably like her own.

She heard, a long way off, someone whisper, "Are they going to sleep forever?" and heard another whisper of "Shhhh." She tried to open her eyes in time to see who was whispering, but the door closed quietly, taking the last bit of light, and she was left alone in the darkness with unspeakable joy in her heart as she realized that she was at last home and safe.

An old fear invaded her thoughts. Her hand moved out in a small circle beneath the sheet, touched Tollie, and the fear disappeared. She smiled in the darkness. They *were* together, safe and together. No matter what had happened, they were home. Secure in this knowledge she dared to stretch and was instantly sorry. Every muscle in her body ached, and there was a slimy taste like castor oil in her mouth. Spots jumped before her eyes and turned into red circles that expanded quickly till they passed out of sight. And while the stomach cramps were not as severe as they had been in the Peppersalt Land, a low, constant nausea had moved in to take their place, a nausea that Slocum had not realized was present until she was aware of food cooking somewhere in the house. Then her stomach turned over with such a thud, such a premature warning that she pinched her lips together as if to hold the sickness back, rolled over on her side, and held her hand over her nose.

Tollie stirred, roused, opened her eyes. From the contortions on her face, Slocum assumed that she was discovering the same areas of distress in her body as she had discovered a few moments earlier. With the thought in mind of offering comfort, Slocum moved closer and whispered, "Guess what? We're home."

Beneath the sheet, Tollie moved her feet up slowly until her knees made a small mountain. She glanced at Slocum, then nodded. "How do you suppose we got here?"

This question had not occurred to Slocum. Somehow it seemed unimportant. They were here, safe in her grandmother's house and that was all that mattered. Feeling rather dumb, she shrugged her shoulders: "Someone must have found us, I guess," she suggested in a small voice.

"And now they're just waiting for us to wake up so they can give us the dickens, I bet." Tollie grew brave and tried to sit up. Her head swayed a little, and a moment later she fell backward as if exhausted. "I feel terrible," she muttered.

They lay in silence after that and listened to the distant sounds of the house. There were footsteps once or twice, as if someone had started up the stairs, then changed her mind. And once they heard a car pull up outside, pause there a moment, then drive on. Tollie's words beat in upon Slocum as she lay there. It had only now occurred to her that everyone from her grandmother on down would be furious with them. Probably someone had called her parents, and they would be here soon to take up the scolding where her grandmother left off. In the thought of facing parental outrage, there was something almost as frightening as her recent experience in the Peppersalt Land. But what it was Slocum could not put into words. She felt as if she had worked very hard on a problem that no one before her had been able to solve. She had brought Tollie back, they were friends once again, and while it was true that the sand pears and ripe plums had had more to do with their reunion than anything else, maybe everyone should suffer mutual stomachaches.

"What do you think we should tell them?" asked Tollie quietly, as if she, too, had been mulling over the future. "You know they'll ask questions—about everything." She sighed deeply. "At least we can tell them the truth about Howard, that we didn't find him and have no idea where he is."

Then, for some reason, Slocum suddenly felt very sorry for Tollie. Obeying an impulse which she did not understand, she leaned over and kissed Tollie on the forehead. It was the first time in her life that she had ever done anything of the kind.

Tollie didn't move. She muttered, "What was that for?"

"I'm just sorry we didn't find Howard," Slocum said. "And I'm doubly sorry about our fight and about all the things I said to you."

Tollie kept her eyes down. "Me, too," she said.

Lying on the bed in the darkness, Slocum gazed on the wide, white expanse of curtain at the window. Two images kept rising in her mind. One was the jolting head of the angry, enraged Howard as he drew back his fist to strike Cicero; the other was of Old Spent Jackson lying peaceful and quiet in his coffin. The memory of Howard, mad, fighting, was painful. The memory of Spent Jackson, who had gained the love of everyone and who was now dead and buried in the cemetery, should have been more painful, yet carried with it a calm sensation that Slocum could not understand.

The phone rang downstairs and the sound carried clearly up to their room. Someone answered it after the first ring. "Are you feeling better now?" Slocum whispered, mostly because it seemed necessary to say something when the silence became awkward with waiting.

"Not particularly. I think I'm just getting used to feeling terrible," joked Tollie. "Do you suppose we'd better call them and get it over with?" she asked, eyeing the door as if behind it was an unspeakable enemy.

"No, they'll come soon enough," said Slocum.

Then in the next minute, as if to confirm Slocum's words, footsteps were heard on the stairs. The girls listened carefully and tried to determine who was coming, and how many of them. It sounded like an army. All the voices were hushed and indistinguishable, and as they came closer the whispering stopped altogether, and left only a deep and profound silence in the hall outside their door.

"We could play dead," Tollie whispered, and pulled the sheet over her head.

Slocum watched the small brass doorknob, waiting for it to turn, anxious in a way for the ordeal to begin so that it would soon be over. She felt Tollie push nearer to her beneath the sheet, reconsidered her suggestion to play dead, and decided instead that if the questions got too difficult that they could always pretend that they were too sick to talk.

The door opened a crack. A face peered into the obscurity of the room beneath the bright light of the hall. The seconds lengthened. Slocum saw her grandmother, now in silhouette, tiptoe softly into the room and stand a few feet away from the bed, looking down intently.

"Are you awake?" she asked gently.

Slocum nodded. The familiar sound of her grandmother's voice, so kind and warm, caused an ominous burning behind the bridge of her nose.

But then her grandmother switched on the small lamp beside the bed and as light spilled out into the dark room, Slocum saw something that made her gasp. Her grandmother was scarcely recognizable. Her white hair was totally disarranged, several strands falling loosely down the side of her face, and her face and dress were grimed heavily as if she had been carrying out ashes, or working in her garden in her best clothes. If Slocum had been in a different mood, she might have gloated over the fact that someone else had been as careless as she had been on occasion, soiling good clothes that Megs would have to work over for hours in order to restore. But Slocum was not in a mood for gloating. She was too shocked at seeing her grandmother thus.

Now she watched her grandmother move carefully around the bed to the other side. "Tollie? Are you in there?" She lifted the sheet and drew it back.

Tollie glanced up, then glanced away, then quickly looked back, as amazed as Slocum by the transformation that had taken place in this woman who firmly believed that cleanliness was not merely next to godliness, but equal to it.

"Well," Grandmother English said, still keeping her voice low. "You both seem to be in one piece, a fact that a great many people are extremely grateful for." She moved to the foot of the bed and made an attempt to straighten one loose strand of hair. "Can you tell me how you feel?"

The direct question took Slocum by surprise, fascinated as she was at seeing such a lack of grooming in her grandmother. She nodded and hoped that a nod would suffice.

"What's that supposed to mean?" smiled Grandmother English. "That you can tell me, or that you are feeling fine?"

Tollie recovered her senses first and looked up in

wary astonishment. "Stomach hurts," she began. Her voice faltered and died away.

"I don't wonder. According to what I heard, you left a trail of plum pits a mile long."

Slocum wanted to ask where she had heard this, but she didn't dare. There was something strained in her grandmother's face that gave a fair indication of deep and prolonged worry. It didn't seem proper somehow now for Slocum to ask questions. She had a feeling that her grandmother had several of her own.

The shuffling of feet could still be heard outside in the hall. Slocum was certain that she heard a man's voice, but it was so low, it was impossible to tell who it was. And there was still this sense coming from the room of a scolding held back, or a lecture, or worse brewing behind her grandmother's tired face.

"Doctor Kate was here," Grandmother English was saying now. "She left some pills that will help you sleep. She said there was not much wrong with either of you that a good night's sleep and a day or two in bed wouldn't cure."

Her kindness, her smudged face and soiled dress all loomed very large before the two girls, who seemed to be making a concentrated effort to become smaller beneath the sheet. If Grandmother English had given them the scolding of their lives, they wouldn't have been either surprised or resentful. They both knew that they deserved one. But she didn't scold; she just sighed and shook her head as she looked at them.

"Somehow, I don't quite feel up to talking any more right now." She smiled apologetically. "And I'm certain that you don't either, although if you have something of importance to tell me, I'll be more than happy to listen."

But even as she said this, she moved slowly toward the door, grasping the edge of the dresser for support. Slocum noticed for the first time that she was without her walking stick. "I'll send Megs in with your medicine," she said, over her shoulder. "Is there anything you want? Something cold to drink?"

Both girls shook their heads as one.

"And you're sure you are feeling all right? No severe pains, no aches?"

Even to this question, they shook their heads in a heartfelt no.

"Well, sleep then. You have visitors, but I'm sure they won't mind coming back in the morning." She switched off the bed light, and in the darkness leaned down and kissed Slocum gently on her forehead. Then she leaned even farther over and kissed Tollie, and her breath sounded thick and labored as she struggled to straighten up. "It's funny," she said, "how wrong the world can seem one evening, and how beautiful and right it can seem the very next. You both are safe and that makes it an altogether right and beautiful world." She moved away from the bed, trailing her voice behind her like music. "Good night, now," she said. The door opened; she slipped out into the light, the room grew quiet, and she was gone.

For a few minutes, neither girl moved. Slocum lay sober and rigid beneath the sheet as if she'd just been given the worst punishment imaginable.

Tollie whispered, "Did you see how she looked?"

"She didn't ask us anything."

All their plans for pretending that they were dead or too sick to talk lay shattered around them. They had been prepared for war, but now they lacked an enemy. They lay in the darkness for a long time, listening to the sounds coming from downstairs. Two more cars arrived, then departed; voices of varying levels and pitch could be heard in the downstairs hall. They thought once about getting out of bed and sneaking to the top of the stairs, but better judgment prevented them from doing this. In a way they felt as miserable, lost, and alone as they had the night before in the Peppersalt Land.

It was wholly dark outside the window when Megs came into the room. She walked on tiptoe like Grandmother English had done, carrying a small tray with an amber-colored bottle and a pitcher dripping moisture and filled with freshly squeezed lemonade. In more ways than one, Slocum was very glad to see her. She felt certain that Megs, unlike her grandmother, would not exercise such self-control, that if she had something on her mind like a scolding or a tongue-lashing, she wouldn't hesitate a minute in delivering it to them.

She wore her best dress, a silk flowered print that she always wore to church on Sunday, and there were small pearl earrings on her ears. With only the briefest of smiles and a scant nod of her head, she placed the pitcher on the nightstand, opened the amber bottle and shook out two white pills, poured two glasses of lemonade and served the whole thing with only three words and a faint smile. "Now take these."

Slocum wanted to scream, "Why is everyone so nice to us? Don't be nice, Megs, bawl us out. It will make everyone feel better."

But, of course, she did no such thing. Slocum sat up in bed along with Tollie, both took the pills, a long deep drink of lemonade, and returned the glasses to Megs' waiting hands, then lay back on their pillows.

"I'm glad you're home," Megs said quietly. "I didn't realize how dull this place can be without you two."

Slocum tried to begin a little apology she had been working on for the last few minutes. She cleared her throat and began shakily. "Megs, Tollie and I—"

Then Megs did an amazing thing: she lifted the tray and walked away toward the door, as if she couldn't care less what Slocum and Tollie had to say. In fact Slocum felt that for some reason Megs didn't even want to stay in the room with them any longer. She acted as if she were following strict orders: "No questions, no answers, just leave them alone."

"Sleep tight now," she called back. The door closed, and she was gone.

Long into the night, in spite of the white pills that were supposed to aid their sleep, the girls lay awake and listened to the variety of noises in the house. The phone rang three times, an unprecedented number of contacts with the outside world for one evening, and there were footsteps in the hall. None of them ever stopped at the bedroom door, but continued on down the hall in the direction of Grandmother English's room.

At last Slocum spoke resolutely, but sleepily. "Tollie, I think we're being punished. I don't think there's anything going on out there, but they want us to think that there is." She looked straight upward at the ceiling.

"We could find out if you want to," whispered Tollie. "We could open the door a crack and—"

But Slocum shook her head. In a way she didn't

want to give them the satisfaction of knowing that this unique form of punishment was working. And in another way, she wasn't certain that it was a device designed to make them curious. Maybe something *was* going on inside her grandmother's house, something as ugly as the fight in Cicero's store, or worse. In either case, she wanted no part of it, not now.

"I guess we'd better go to—" But she never finished. Sleep came, suddenly, drastically, cutting short her advice for the future. And with sleep came dreams that were almost as lonely, almost as frightening as the dreams she had suffered the night before in the Peppersalt Land.

FIFTEEN

THEY STAYED IN their room and in their bed for two days and two nights. And during this time they were treated to a small parade of visitors and well-wishers. Megs came more often than anyone else, bringing syrup that soothed their throats, the results of bad summer colds that had set in after their night in the Peppersalt Land.

And others came as well. There was stern Doctor Kate who poked and prodded, and looked down at them over the rims of her glasses as if she didn't know what to do first, scold them or heal them. And two women from Budding Grove came, friends of Grandmother English, bringing a beautiful bouquet of pink carnations and white roses and warm smiles and urgent instructions for the girls to get well so the whole town could enjoy the sight of them playing together on Grandmother English's broad front lawn. Two of Tollie's school friends came and spoke only to Tollie in low hushed tones, and eyed Slocum in a way that made her feel embarrassed. And once Mr. Cicero came and left them each a bag of jawbreakers and bubble gum with the advice that the girls turn the candy over to Megs to be dispensed when she saw fit.

People came and went but no one stayed long enough to answer any of their most persistent questions. And Megs was always there, as if standing guard at the door, listening, ushering the visitors out almost as soon as they entered.

Grandmother English did little more than stick her head in the door three or four times a day. And while her appearance had changed in that the smudges were gone from her face and her dress was fresh and clean as always, there was still something worried and tense in her expression. She never questioned them about their night in the Peppersalt Land, and never gave them a chance to ask questions of their own such as who had found them, and brought them to safety, and that most important question of all, where was Howard Jackson? They were simply treated to endless smiles and sympathy, doses of medicine, and closed doors.

As their frustration increased with the confinement, their tempers grew short. They argued over who had the most of the sheet, whose pillow was well beyond the center of the bed, who had the biggest piece of gingerbread, and finally the biggest argument of all, whose fault was it that they had come home at all, and not proceeded on in search of Howard.

"We might have been in Atlanta by now," said Tollie, "instead of here being held prisoners."

"We're not prisoners," grumbled Slocum, something less than conviction in her voice. "And as I remember it, you were the one who came back."

"Just because I was sick," muttered Tollie. "And if you hadn't suggested that we eat those pears—"

"I suggested it," flared Slocum. "I was the one who warned you about eating stuff that you didn't know about."

At last Tollie sat up straight in bed and threw back the sheet. "Well, I'm not staying here any longer."

"What do you mean?" asked Slocum, alarmed. She scowled at Tollie. She remembered very clearly their fight in the Peppersalt Land and the things they had said to each other. "Don't be silly," she went on, as if to comfort her. And then she added quickly, "The very next person who comes in this room will stay and talk to us, even if we have to . . . " She broke off, unable to think of what they might have to do in order to demand the attention they wanted.

"It won't do any good," said Tollie. "I have a feeling they're going to keep us here until we're old gray-haired women because they're afraid to let us out."

"Afraid?"

Tollie didn't explain. Still poised on the side of the bed, she looked uncertain and angry.

Softly now, coming up the stairs, they heard footsteps. They listened for a moment, heard the sound coming in the direction of their room. Then quickly, Tollie crawled back beneath the sheet. Together they lay side by side, breath held, their eyes trained on the door, ready to do whatever was necessary to detain this new visitor long enough to answer some questions.

The door opened a crack. Megs' face appeared. "Are you asleep?" She stood back and opened the door wider. "You have a very special visitor." She smiled.

A moment later, Mary Jackson entered the room. Her eyes were red, and she had a wan smile on her face and her hair seemed streaked with new gray. She brought the girls two small coloring books and a box of crayons and gave them instructions to share the crayons. She looked as sad and lost now as when the girls had last seen her, the day of Spent Jackson's funeral.

"You caused us some grief we didn't need," she said, sadly, standing a distance from the bed. Then her round face broke into a semblance of a smile. "But you're safe now, and that's all that counts."

It was a moment of considerable sadness as the girls remembered the funeral, remembered the fact that Mary had had to endure it alone. Slocum thought of a hundred things to say, but she could not muster the courage to ask the simplest of all questions, "Where's Howard?" Instead she thanked Mary politely for the coloring books, although the gift really would have been more appropriate for someone much younger than herself. And Tollie thanked her in the same fashion, thumbing through the pages filled with drawings of blank-looking children bouncing balls and playing with puppies.

Then there was Megs again, telling Mary that they needed their rest, and that she'd better go now.

Mary came close to the bed and looked down on the girls. She gave them a heartbreaking smile and whispered, "You oughtn't never go in that place again, you hear? Old Spent used to say that's the devil's land, not fit for human folk."

Slocum grew brave. She grasped Mary Jackson's hand and held on as if for life. "I'm sorry about Old Spent," she said, ". . . and I'm sorry that Howard . . ." She paused, hoping that Mary would hear the name and volunteer some information.

But if she had anything at all to tell the girls, she elected to keep quiet. In fact the mention of Howard's name only seemed to make her feel worse. She patted Slocum's hand and turned quickly away from the bed, as if on the verge of tears. She didn't even stop to say good-bye, but instead hurried to the door and out of it.

Megs lingered long enough to tell them that she would be up in a little while with their medicine. Then, she too was gone, and the girls were left alone again.

Suddenly Tollie sat up on the edge of the bed, strong with resolution. "Get dressed," she ordered. "We're going downstairs."

Slocum nodded in complete agreement and scurried out of bed. Together they threw on their clothes, made an attempt to straighten their hair, which had grown mussed and tangled during their confinement in bed, took a brief last look in the mirror, then ventured quietly toward the door, as if they *were* prisoners plotting an escape.

At the top of the stairs, they stopped, listening.

There were voices coming from the living room. They recognized Grandmother English's voice, and Megs', and Mary Jackson was there, as well as two men. At first the voices were so soft that the girls couldn't hear what was being said. They ventured halfway down the stairs, keeping close to the wall.

"I think, Sheriff Paul," they heard Grandmother English say, "that it would be best if you didn't come out here anymore. I should think there would be enough work for you in Budding Grove without having to run out here looking for trouble."

"I'm not looking for trouble, Mrs. English. I'm simply doing my job. I have a citizen here with a reasonable complaint, and I have reason to believe that the offender is somewhere near or on your property."

There was a pause. Slocum had never heard her grandmother speak so coldly. "Do you have a search warrant, Sheriff Paul?"

"No, I didn't think that was necessary."

"Oh, indeed it *is* necessary. And you'll find out how necessary it is from my lawyer if you dare set foot on my property again."

The next voice they recognized as Cicero's. "I got damages in my store," he said, "to say nothing of my own personal injuries."

"I told you I would be happy to pay any amount that was reasonable."

"But Mrs. English, that's not the point, and that's not getting to the root of the problem," protested Sheriff Paul.

"The problem was one of your own making, Sheriff Paul. There's no problem here now that I can see."

"Well, look at it this way," said Sheriff Paul. "If you're harboring a criminal—"

But that's all he had a chance to say, because suddenly the girls heard Grandmother English's voice, as strong, as firm, as unbending as they had ever heard it.

"If I'm harboring a criminal," she began, placing special emphasis on the last word, "I'd only be giving protection to a young man who was goaded into a fight that he didn't want in the first place, and you know it, Cicero, as well as I do, and if you elect to do something about it, then we'll take it to court and let Tollie and Slocum tell the jury exactly what did happen. And if I am harboring a criminal, I would only be giving protection to a young man who knows his history much better than either of you, knows that the white man's justice seldom if ever extends itself to the black man. And I for one would like to prove to him, if I'm given another chance, that there *is* hope for the future, that the days and months ahead will be better than the ones behind. And if either of you had an ounce of sense in your heads, you'd see that if the future is not better for the Howard Jacksons of the world, it's not going to be any better for you either."

Her voice echoed throughout the house, filling each corner with the conviction of her beliefs. She spoke as if she were saying something that she'd wanted to say for a long time. Slocum felt goose-bumps on her arms. Together the girls sat halfway down the stairs, listening, wondering how it would all end.

Sheriff Paul coughed, as if out of embarrassment at this new turn of events. "Very pretty speech, Mrs. English, but the fact remains that—"

"What fact, Sheriff Paul?"

"There are charges against Howard Jackson."

"What charges?"

Slocum and Tollie made an effort to hold still on the steps, aware that the slightest noise would betray them.

There was a pause as if Sheriff Paul were having to sort through the various charges in his mind, or else invent a few. "Mrs. English, you're not being reasonable," he said, finally.

"Perhaps I'm not. But if you ask me, both of you gentlemen have only one real grievance against Howard Jackson. And that happens to be something over which he has no control."

"What are you referring to, Mrs. English?"

"The color of his skin."

There was a tense silence coming from the living room. Slocum tried to hold her breath, afraid that she was breathing too loudly. Tollie caught her attention, and grinned broadly, her dark eyes dancing with delight at what was being said in the living room.

Then there was a scuffle of chairs being scraped across the floor, and a man's sullen promise that "This business isn't over yet, Mrs. English."

"It's completely over as far as I'm concerned. You gentlemen are always welcome in my house as long as you do not come to persecute and hound me or my friends." Suddenly Grandmother English's voice had grown as warm and musical as if she were bidding guests good night for the evening. "Give my regards to your wife, Mr. Cicero. And if you'll mail me a list of repairs as well as any medical services that you might have incurred, I'll have a check in the mail for you the following day."

The living room doors opened. Tollie and Slocum realized too late that they had lingered too long. There was no chance for escape. All they could do was sit very still and hope that they blended with the carpet and woodwork.

Sheriff Paul and Cicero led the way, hats in hand, followed by Grandmother English, then Megs, then Mary Jackson. At the door, Cicero stopped. "Is Howard Jackson here in your house right now, Mrs. English?"

Grandmother English started to answer, but Megs rushed in. "Now why would you be asking a silly question like that?" She ducked her head and walked rapidly to the door as if to speed their departure.

Cicero grinned and shook his head. "Never thought I'd live to see the day that the English place was turned into a hide-out for—"

"For what, Mr. Cicero?" The icy quality had returned to Grandmother English's voice. She straightened her shoulders and asked again, "For what?"

Cicero returned her gaze for a moment. Then he shrugged his shoulders and brushed past Sheriff Paul and disappeared onto the front porch.

Sheriff Paul hesitated a moment longer. He fingered the brim of his hat constantly and kept his eyes down. "I'm not certain any of us handled this the right way, Mrs. English."

"I don't think there is a right way and a wrong way any longer, Sheriff Paul. A great many of us have been negligent and remiss for too many years. And now times are changing, and rightly so. All we can do is make an effort to keep up with them and try to alter and improve our way of looking at people. *All* people!" There was sadness in her voice now, a fatigue that reminded Slocum of the disheveled, smudged woman who had first visited their room three days ago. Now she shook Sheriff Paul's hand as warmly as if no harsh words had been exchanged between them. He bobbed his head and muttered, "G'night, Ma'am," and hurried off into the night.

Megs waited at the living room door, her cheeks flushed, a broad grin across her face. "You handled that very well, Mrs. English. I couldn't have done better myself."

But Mary Jackson's face was a mask of bewilderment. She stared, eyes wide, at both women. A question seemed to be forming on her lips, but it took her forever to find enough voice to go with it. Finally, "Is—is Howard . . .?" she whispered, and her voice broke as she looked searchingly from one woman to the other.

Grandmother English shook her head sadly. But before she had a chance to speak, Megs stepped forward. She fidgeted constantly with the hem of her apron, and looked as confused and remorseful as Slocum had ever seen her. "I'm—sorry, Mrs. English. But I was afraid to tell you. I didn't know how you stood on—things—until a few moments ago. Howard came here shortly after they found the girls. He wanted to know how they were. He didn't want to stay, but I made him. I hid him in the attic."

For a moment, Grandmother English's face was completely without expression. Then slowly she smiled. "Well, where is he?"

Without a word, Megs walked quickly, quietly across the hall and knocked lightly on the doors that led into the dining room.

A moment later the doors opened, and there in

the bright light of the hall stood a very dirty, very ragged Howard Jackson. He took a few steps toward his mother, then stopped as if aware and embarrassed by his appearance. His hand stroked the stubble of black beard, while the other hand moved up toward his grimed forehead. "I'm—I'm sorry," he said, faltering.

But that was all he said, because suddenly Mary Jackson ran to him and took him in her arms. She pressed both hands against the side of his face as if to hold it steady so that she might look at it for a long time. She was weeping and seemed not to notice that her tears were mingling with the dirt on his face. All she did was weep and hold him, and murmur continuously, "Spent's dead, Spent's dead." And Howard answered her in a mournful, plaintive counterpoint of "I know, Mary, I know," and hugged her close to him.

Slocum watched the reunion through blurred eyes and heard Tollie sniffle and saw Megs turn away. Presently Grandmother English said quietly to Megs, "Fix two rooms for them at the end of the hall. They'll stay here tonight."

"We can't do that, Mrs. English," protested Mary Jackson through her tears. "You've done enough—"

"I've done nothing," she replied. "There's plenty of room in this big house."

Howard took a step forward, his face suddenly strong in spite of the stubble of beard and smudges. "No charity, please, Mrs. English. I'm not very good with a hoe, and—"

"Who said anything about a hoe, Howard, and who said anything about charity?" Slocum was a little shocked at the tone of voice her grandmother used with Howard. It varied little from the tone she had recently used with Cicero and Sheriff Paul. She appeared to be beyond discussing anything with anyone at the moment, and said as much with the next breath. "Now, I want everyone to go upstairs and get some sleep. Megs will show you the—"

Suddenly she glanced in the direction of the stairs. Her eyes squinted at the two small shadowy figures perched midway on the steps. As she passed beneath the light in the hall, Slocum saw something in her face as stern and unbending as her voice. "Eavesdropping," she began, "is considered by some to be a criminal activity."

Tollie cleared her throat and moved closer to Slocum. "We really weren't eavesdropping," she said. "Everybody was talking so loud, we could practically hear everything in our room." Tollie looked directly at Howard now, a beautiful, warm smile on her face. "Besides, Howard's back," she announced, as if no one else had eyes to see.

The stern expression on Grandmother English's face softened. "So he is," she said. "Well, aren't you going to say hello to him?"

And that was all Tollie needed. She flew down the steps and hugged Howard with such force that both of them almost lost their balance. Slocum followed a little more hesitantly, but by the time she was at his side, his arm was opened to her, and she slipped beneath it and pressed close to his side.

"We looked and looked for you," said Slocum.

"I know," he said, and looked embarrassed, and left the sentence unfinished.

Grandmother English stared at the three of them for a long moment. Then she roused herself and walked stiffly, erectly toward the living room door. "Now, everybody go to bed and leave me alone for awhile.

We'll talk in the morning."

Mary Jackson tried to protest once more, but Megs would hear none of it. She ushered her up the stairs with strict instructions for Howard and the girls to follow.

Slocum stayed a moment longer. She looked closely at her grandmother standing alone at the living room door. It struck her that she looked much older that evening, tired, less animated. She noticed that the lines on her face were becoming wider, deeper. But she also noticed that her eyes were peaceful, as if she had at last solved some ancient mystery, or else was relieved of carrying some intolerable burden a step further. Slocum went over and kissed her lightly and noticed that her face brightened as if she were pleased.

"I'm sorry for all the trouble we've caused you," Slocum said.

"Sometimes it's difficult to tell who exactly starts trouble," smiled her grandmother. "Problems grow, and we don't always have the kind of wisdom necessary for the solution of them. We'll try to do better in the future. Now you need your sleep."

Tollie started toward the stairs, her arm still around Howard's waist. At the first step, she stopped. She glanced back at Grandmother English, standing alone at the living room door, then suddenly she ran to her, and threw her arms around her. "I love you," she whispered.

Grandmother English looked surprised. Then she kissed her and held her tightly, turning her face away.

Slocum started up the stairs first. Howard followed, head down. Tollie stayed behind, her arms tightly entwined around her grandmother's neck.

SIXTEEN

ALL THE WAY UP the stairs, Slocum tried to figure out a way that she and Tollie could be alone with Howard for a few minutes. But no device, no plan, no idea came to her that would escape Megs' sharp eye. Then in front of their bedroom door, the problem took care of itself. Howard waved his mother and Megs ahead with the terse announcement, "You two go along. I'll be there in a minute."

Megs started to object, but Mary Jackson took her by the arm, as if *she* were leading the way. Tollie and Slocum grinned with delight, then seized Howard by the hands, and dragged him into their room. Tollie closed the door and leaned against it as if she were afraid that Megs might appear at any moment and demand that Howard leave. After all, this had been her pattern for three days, and Megs was not one to break a pattern easily.

With the door closed, the girls gave way to a deluge of questions; they tumbled out, one after the other, both talking at once, an expression of feverish excitement on their faces.

"What happened?"

"Where were you? We looked and—"

"We left some food. Did you find it?"

But all this time, Howard kept moving slowly, but steadily away toward the center of the room, his head down, his hands laced behind his back. Suddenly he whirled around, his face contorted by anger, his voice as steady and measured as his step. "Now just a minute," he began, "I didn't come in here to answer questions. I came in here to ask a few of my own." He commenced pacing, glancing up now and then at the girls who stood close by the door, shocked at the unexpected outburst.

"First of all," he said, and again his voice and face gave the impression of just barely controlled fury. "Whatever possessed you two to pull such a stupid trick? And second, do you have any idea, any conception of the worry and anxiety you caused everyone? Did you think you were going on a picnic? Were you at all aware of the hazards and dangers you were subjecting yourselves to? Hadn't you been told time and time again never to go near the Peppersalt Land?"

During this barrage of questions, his voice rose.

He stopped pacing and stood now in a direct confrontation with the two girls. His eyes were extraordinarily hard and seemed to see nothing but offenses and offenders.

Tollie blinked her eyes and continually fidgeted with the door knob behind her. She muttered, "We just thought that—"

"You didn't think at all," interrupted Howard. "That's the whole point. Couldn't you muster enough common sense between you to talk yourselves out of such a stupid trick?"

Slocum felt that he was being unfair. She tried to get a word in. "You asked us to help—"

"Not that way, I didn't," he declared. Again he started walking back and forth in front of them, pointing his finger. "All I asked you to do was to come on back here and tell your grandmother exactly what had happened, to tell the truth precisely as you knew it, that's all. I didn't ask you to go wandering off into that hellhole without food and water, without telling anyone where you were going, without any sense of direction, without any sense at all, apparently."

For a moment he seemed overcome by his own fury. He stared at the girls, and shook his head. "Good Lord," he went on, "why do you think everyone told you over and over again to stay out of there? Did you think that your grandmother just enjoyed giving you those orders?" He shoved his hands in his pockets, and repeated himself very slowly. "All I asked you to do was come back here and tell the truth. That's all."

Tollie edged away from the door, as if she were equally as fed up. She looked half-mad, and half-hurt. "Well, we did that," she protested, weakly, "but it didn't seem like much."

"Oh, but you're wrong, Tollie. Telling the truth is a great deal, perhaps the most important thing a person can do. And sometimes it's very difficult." Howard lifted his head. For just a moment, just a split second, Slocum thought he looked exactly like Old Spent. Again he turned away and rubbed the back of his neck, and shook his head. "I've a good mind to blister you both," he muttered, "like your grandmother should have done three days ago."

Slocum felt her heart beating in her throat. She nudged Tollie and motioned toward the bed. Quietly they slipped behind Howard and crawled beneath the sheet. The slight rustling caught his attention, and he turned on them again, his face more relaxed. "Now, I want both of you to promise me something," he said, coming straight to the foot of the bed and pointing his finger at them. "I want you to promise, both of you, on your word of honor that you'll never again go into the Peppersalt Land. Do you understand?"

Both girls nodded meekly and burrowed deeper into the covers.

"The place ought to be blown off the face of the earth if you ask me," he added, "but that's your grandmother's business, not mine. But I *can* make your safety my business, and if either of you had any idea how close you were to real danger, you'd think long and hard about it before you stepped a foot in there again. Do you hear?"

They heard. There was a new somberness on his face now that impressed the girls. But there was still a stubborn streak in Tollie. "People lived there once," she said. "You told me so yourself. If it's so dangerous for us, why wasn't it dangerous for—"

"Not by choice, Tollie. They didn't live there by choice." All that could be said of his face now was that it was wholly grim. "And that's another thing," he went on, flaring again, as if a whole new opportunity for scolding had suddenly appeared before him. "Slocum's right," he declared. "I've been talking too much, and you've been listening too much, Tollie, listening to all the wrong things."

Slocum looked up, her mind whirling. She remembered the harsh words she'd exchanged with Tollie in the Peppersalt Land. But she'd said them to Tollie alone. There wasn't anyone else present to hear. "How—how did you know I said that?" she asked.

For the first time since Howard had come into their room, his face softened. He opened his mouth, then closed it again, and walked slowly, as if he were deep in thought, around the bed, then back to his original position. "I heard," he said and quickly ducked his head to avoid the close scrutiny of the girls.

"But how could you unless . . . " Slocum broke off and exchanged a puzzled glance with Tollie.

Howard made a despairing gesture and stared thoughtfully out of the window at the night. "I tried to scare you away," he said. "Good grief, how I tried. I screeched and howled until I thought I'd wake the dead."

Slowly Tollie sat up in bed. "You mean the night we left the thermos . . . "

Slocum remembered the unearthly screeching that had sent them fleeing from the edge of the Peppersalt Land toward the safety of the house. "Was—was that you?" she asked.

Howard nodded and continued looking out of

the window. From the new tone in his voice, the girls could only assume that he was smiling. "I'll say this for both of you. You don't scare easily."

Tollie was on her knees now on the bed, trying to piece the mystery together. "Then you knew about Old Spent?"

Howard bowed his head and leaned against the top of the window. He nodded slowly and said nothing.

"And you saw us when we went into the Peppersalt Land?" Slocum asked incredulously. "You—were watching us all the time?"

It seemed forever before Howard even moved. He continued to stand by the window and lean against it, saying nothing as if all the wearisome activity of the last few days had left him too exhausted for further talk. Finally he roused himself and walked slowly back to the bed. He pulled a chair close and sat down.

All this time the girls watched him with a degree of intensity that knew no bounds. Slocum remembered the sound of footsteps, the rustle of twigs cracking, the sensation that someone was watching them. When she was certain that Howard had no intention of answering her question, she asked another one, very softly, almost afraid to hear the answer. "If you were there all the time, why didn't you help us?"

Something unaccountable was going on in Howard. He rubbed his eyes and left his hands shading his face. "Because you both were helping me," he said, finally. The summer evening outside of the window was alive with locusts; their chorus filled the room as if to comfort them with their song. Howard raised his head. His eyes were shining. He appeared to be listening to the tangible beauty of the hour. "You both taught me so much," he said softly. "Your words, the things you said to each other, your obvious love and concern for each other." He paused and grinned broadly. "Even your fight. What a fight!"

He leaned back in the chair and rested his head. "I wasn't going to let anything happen to you, but I had to watch. I had to see what you did. And I saw, and heard enough to know that I've been wrong about a number of things."

Slocum and Tollie sat quietly, listening, not always understanding, but aware that something important, something to be remembered was being said to them. Howard was sitting there before them, smiling at them, thanking them for teaching him something, although they weren't certain what.

"Then you're the one who found us?" Slocum asked.

Howard shook his head. "No, but you might say I led the way. I had help. There were several rescue parties out. Even old Cicero was helping."

He stood up now, as if he were leaving. Both girls moved as one to delay his departure. "Don't go yet," Tollie pleaded.

Howard looked at his shirt and rubbed his beard, as if embarrassed. "I'd better. Look at me!"

"Where're you going? What are you going to do tomorrow?"

He stopped at the door and appeared to be studying the doorknob. "I don't know. I'll probably take Mary home and get her settled, then it might be best if I leave here for awhile."

Both girls protested. Deep wrinkles formed on their foreheads, and their eyes were worried. "Are you going back to school, Howard?" Slocum asked.

There was no answer.

Now the door was opened, and Howard was standing halfway out into the hall. His voice sounded light, but his eyes were clouded. He called back a final piece of advice. "Don't worry about tomorrow. It'll be here soon enough. Get some sleep."

Then he was gone.

Late that night, Slocum and Tollie heard footsteps move past their door, heading in the direction of the small staircase that led to the attic. Sometime later they heard them coming back again. There were muffled voices and the scuffle of feet, then the noise faded down the steps, and all was quiet.

"What do you suppose is happening now?" whispered Tollie.

Slocum shook her head. She wished that she could have complete confidence in the future, but the past few days had shown her that life sometimes held brutal surprises. She tried to close her eyes and force sleep to come. But the mysterious late night activity bothered her. The remembrance of Howard's face and the uncertainty of tomorrow stuck in her mind. She remembered her grandmother's strange words about problems and the wisdom to solve them, and nothing she remembered seemed to make any sense at all.

She tried to stay awake long enough to see how the night would end. She studied the darkness as if in a dream, feeling new anxieties and fears arise within her, yet lacking the energy and wisdom to deal with them.

SEVENTEEN

MORNINGS IN Budding Grove were always pretty much alike, dreadfully routine with the air hanging still and hot and heavy. But on this morning everything was different. The girls awakened to the sound of a man's voice coming from the kitchen.

Tollie sat up, puzzled. "What in the . . . ?"

Slocum went to the door and opened it a crack. There was no one to be seen, but the voice persisted. Then the fragrant odor of pecan waffles drifted beneath their door.

"Mary Jackson's cooking," grinned Slocum.

"And Howard's here," remembered Tollie.

Moving at top speed, the girls left the bed, dressed and ran downstairs.

In the kitchen they found Megs and Mary Jackson bent over the stove, while Grandmother English sat at the table before a steaming cup of coffee, talking to Howard who stood by the window gazing out in the direction of the Peppersalt Land. Apparently they had been having a very earnest conversation about something. Now as the girls appeared, they both fell silent.

"I was beginning to think you were going to sleep all day," said Grandmother English, obviously changing the subject. "Now sit down and eat your breakfast."

There was a tone in her voice that left no margin for disagreement. Slocum and Tollie sat on either side of the table, hands folded.

Throughout the meal everyone looked very serene and detached, as if nothing at all unusual was going on. Mary Jackson and Megs chatted lightly about menus and exchanged recipes for corn bread. And Howard ate six waffles, and seemed to brood continuously, as if he were facing an insoluble problem.

Finally the meal was over, and there at the end of the table was Grandmother English, stiffly erect, poised, and confident as ever, the lines of fatigue less visible on her face than the night before. She took a final sip of coffee, dabbed primly at her lips with her napkin, folded it evenly, then pushed back from the table, and said,

"Now! I want to show you something."

Slocum and Tollie looked at each other, wary,

wondering what new surprise was in store for them.

Grandmother English started toward the door that led into the dining room. Mary Jackson and Megs agreed to let the dishes wait for awhile and followed after her. Howard stayed in his chair.

"Aren't you coming?" asked Grandmother English.

Slowly, begrudgingly, Howard pushed away from the table and muttered something about how late it was.

Grandmother English said, "It will only take a minute."

The girls exchanged a cautious glance. Slocum wondered if this was some new sort of punishment. Slowly they left the table and ventured as far as the dining room door. There they stopped, seeing, but not believing the most amazing spectacle that greeted their eyes.

There before them on the dining room table was a large flat board, and on the board someone had constructed an exquisitely beautiful model village. The small houses were dusty, and some of the paint was chipping here and there, but the skill with which they had been constructed was obvious to all. Delicate church spires rose soaring above smaller buildings, and tiny striped awnings hung gracefully suspended on toothpick-sized standards. A few of the structures had been labeled with miniature signs, the Ice Cream Shoppe, the Green Grocer, the Hardware Store, and there was one central boulevard dotted with small green shrubs and multicolored flowers no larger than the head of a pin. Between the small buildings ran dainty gravel pathways, interlacing the community and giving the entire spectacle the fragile aura of a dream. Each building was complete even down to the miniature glass windowpanes and red brick chimneys. Every detail had been lovingly attended to and perfectly executed.

Grandmother English came up close between them, laid an arm gently on each of their shoulders. "Well, what do you think?" she asked, in a matter-of-fact tone. "Howard built this a long time ago."

Slocum and Tollie studied the model from every angle, each pointing out some small detail that the other one had overlooked. It was far too complex to take in at a glance, and it was perfect.

Slocum could find no words. Finally she stammered, "It's—beautiful."

All this time, Howard had stayed back by the door. Now he moved slowly toward the table, as if seeing the model for the first time. On his face there was a curious expression, a mixture of embarrassment and pleasure. "Where did you find this?" he asked, his voice scarcely audible.

Grandmother English answered quickly, simply, "Mary wanted to keep it, of course, but she didn't have room to store it. I offered the corner of our attic. It's been there all this time."

Now Megs and Mary Jackson moved close to the table and for a moment they all stood quietly, studying the model, admiring the obvious artistry that had gone into its construction.

Grandmother English was the first to stir. "It occurred to me last night," she began, "that after the chaos of the last few days, it might do us all good for a change to focus on something of beauty and order."

The girls watched her anxiously, wondering, and sometimes worrying about the look that crossed her face as she spoke. Suddenly she was so serious, enclosing them in her arms, yet talking straight ahead, as if she were speaking to the walls, the ceiling.

"It occurred to me several nights ago when you two were lost in that terrible place that if anything happened to you it would be my fault. The injustice of the past doesn't go away by fencing it off. Quite the contrary. It grows by what it feeds on and becomes as tangled and impassable, as ugly as the Peppersalt Land."

Her voice fell very low and her eyes had a dim, glazed look about them, as if she were staring a hundred years back into the past. She moved to the window and stared out at the green desolation of the Peppersalt Land. "There is a land lying in destruction," she said, bobbing her head, "both physical and spiritual. If the twisted paths and rusted pieces of tin and creepers and thorns and all the hideous memories—if all that could be buried and forgotten, how simple it would be. But it can't. Life has to take the place of the death that occurred there, and life requires human beings, people, you, me, all of us, we have to work together and cover the old scars with new growth."

She paused and looked down at the earnest young faces of her listeners. "I'm not certain that I've put it in a way that you'll understand," she explained after a moment. "I'm not certain that I understand it fully myself. It's more a feeling than a knowing. Do you know what I mean?"

Slocum and Tollie nodded quietly. There were, indeed, some things that she had said that they could not comprehend. But it was still nice having her talk so seriously to them, as if she were entrusting something to them of great value.

Howard stood quietly beside the model. He said nothing, gave no indication that he had even heard what was being said. Slowly he circled the table, all the time staring down. Softly he said, "It needs paint."

"Then paint it!" said Grandmother English, firmly.

"It's dusty—"

"Then clean it!"

"I was just a kid—"

"True," said Grandmother English, "but you were a kid with an enormous talent for building things. The world has always needed builders, Howard, but I don't suppose there has ever been a time when we needed them more than we need them now. Any fool can destroy. But it takes rare courage and talent to build."

She paused for a moment and drew a deep breath. "You have time to restore the model completely—" She hesitated, then seemed to draw a deeper breath; she added softly but firmly, "before you go back to school."

Suddenly a taut look crossed Howard's face. He stared at Grandmother English for a long time without speaking. Slocum thought that he looked almost as mad as he looked that day in Cicero's store. Once or twice he started to speak, but seemed to change his mind. Finally he said, "It'll take work."

"Some," agreed Grandmother English, "but then anything worthwhile takes work, wouldn't you agree, Howard?"

He looked her straight in the eye, his head erect, as if he were meeting a challenge. The look in his eye pleased Slocum and Tollie. They grasped his hands, as if they did not want him to return to the sullen, angry Howard of last week, as if they wanted to remove all possibilities of a return to shadows and nightmares.

"We'll help, if you let us," Slocum said timidly.

"Hope we don't ruin it for you," gulped Tollie, still very much in awe of the craftsmanship of the model.

It seemed forever before Howard spoke. He stood for a long time staring down at the model. There was something in his face which made Slocum wonder if he was seeing the model at all. Finally he said, "All right," and that was all, but that was enough.

Megs went into the kitchen for a pan of warm soapy water and soft cloths. Slocum and Tollie ran upstairs in search of paintbrushes and paint. When they came back down, they saw Mary Jackson sitting to one side of the table watching Howard, her face as calm and relaxed as Slocum had ever seen it. Grandmother English stood by the window, looking out, her head bowed, her hands clasped behind her.

All morning and well into the afternoon, the three of them worked over the model, mending, cleaning, restoring, applying fresh paint with tiny paintbrushes. Late in the afternoon Howard seemed to lose interest in the project. He raised up from the close work, as if to straighten a painful kink out of his back; he looked around, and adjusted his shirt, and wiped his hands on a cloth, and without a word walked out of the room.

Tollie and Slocum glanced at each other. They heard the front door open, then close, and a moment later, they caught sight of Howard walking up and down beside the fence that bordered the Peppersalt Land. He seemed to be pacing, his head down, as if he were deep in thought.

"Come on, let's go," whispered Tollie.

They were out the front door and halfway down the steps when Grandmother English appeared behind the screen. "Just a moment," she called, "where are you going?"

"To get Howard," Slocum replied.

Grandmother English came all the way out of the door. She looked closely at the girls for a moment. "I think it would be best to leave him alone."

"Why?" Tollie protested. "We just want to help—"

Grandmother English looked stern but kind. "Maybe he needs your help in some matters, Tollie, but not in all. Leave him alone for now, please."

Slocum started to protest, but changed her mind. Slowly they returned to the dining room, and took up their paintbrushes, always keeping an eye on Howard outside the window, walking up and down, up and down beside the Peppersalt Land.

Fragments of thoughts drifted through Slocum's head. She heard her grandmother's voice in memory, "Life has to take the place of the death that has occurred here." And she heard Howard's voice, "My soul and thy soul." She would never forget that as long as she lived.

The sun was almost down now. It would be night soon. Shadows filled the corners of the room. Slocum's back ached from bending over. Everything that had happened had left her almost as confused as before. But she knew now that there were a few very important things to remember, and a few things to forget, and so much to work for.

She knew that, somehow, she and Tollie had to convince them that there was so much to work for.

Somehow, she had to convince them.